This is a work of fiction. Character names and descriptions are the product of the author's imagination. Any resemblance to actual persons, living or dead is entirely coincidental

Cover By Cherish Creations

Edited By Alicia Ramos

ISBN Number 978-1-7367906-9-4

Published By Penning Purposefully ®

Acknowledgments

This author journey has truly been bittersweet. I have been walking in this author space for 15 years, growing, learning, stretching, and evolving with every book. Fiction has always had a special place in my heart, and Nicole's Story, released in 2015, was the last fiction book I wrote until now.

Writing this story reminded me why I started telling stories in the first place. Stories have power. They allow us to see ourselves, heal, reflect, and sometimes just escape for a moment.

I am deeply grateful to every reader who has supported my work, shared my books, encouraged me, and continued to believe in the stories I carry. Your support means more than you know. Most importantly, I thank God for the gift and ability to tell stories with purpose. I never take that lightly, and I'm grateful for every opportunity to put words on a page and share them with the world.

Dedication

To every girl who has ever felt alone in the world like Brielle, I see you. You are not your past. Your story is still being written, and your future is greater than anything that tried to break you.

The Streets Don't Love Me Like She Does

By MzSheriBaby

Table of Contents

Chapter One

Tremaine Williams aka Stacks kicked back in the VIP section, elbow resting on the leather booth, eyes scanning the lounge like he owned the place. His best friend's, Darius aka Brick, birthday party had the bottles coming faster than the waitresses could pour, and the music was loud enough to shake the glass.

Women hovered. Always did. He didn't care what they said as long as they let him fuck. However, he was not satisfied. Lately, he was feeling like something in his life was missing. He had just about everything he wanted, so he didn't know where this feeling was coming from but tonight, he didn't want to think about it.

One leaned in close enough for him to feel her breath.

"Anybody ever tell you look like Trey Songz?"

He smirked without looking at her.

"Anybody ever tell you that flattery don't get you nowhere?"

She laughed anyway and kept it moving. Bees to honey. Same old.

He took a sip of his drink and frowned slightly. That feeling hit him again. The quiet one. The one that didn't care how many bottles popped or how many numbers landed in his phone. He had money. Status. Options. Still, he felt like something was off.

Not tonight, though. Tonight was about noise and distraction. Michelle was the chosen girl for the night. Caramel thick, lashes dramatic, attitude loud. She looked good on his arm but that's where it stopped. Too much talk. Too many rules. The type that wanted cash first and energy never.

He wasn't new to the game.

A lot of dudes fell for that tease-and-bleed routine. Tremaine wasn't one of them. If he wanted a woman, he had one. If he didn't, he didn't force it. Michelle had already talked herself out of ever being an option.

Then someone tapped his shoulder.

He turned. Redbone. Pretty. Pink dress hugging her like it knew what it was doing. She leaned closer, lips moving, but the music swallowed her words.

He tilted his head. "Come here."

She stepped in, and her perfume hit him. Clean. Soft. Dangerous.

"Damn," he muttered before he could stop himself.

She smiled at him seductively. "You want to dance?"

He chuckled, slow and amused. "I don't dance."

She raised a brow. "So, you just gonna sit up here lookin' fine all night?"

That got him. He studied her now. Confident. Mouth slick. Not begging.

"What's your name?"

She smirked and stepped back. "Why don't you come find out?"

And just like that, she turned and walked off.

Tremaine watched her go, eyes dragging shamelessly. That ass in that pink dress was disrespectful.

He lifted his glass, shaking his head. "I ain't chasin' no chick," he muttered. "She must be out her damn mind."

Still, his eyes followed her until she disappeared into the crowd.

He leaned back and finally noticed that Michelle was nowhere to be found. Good. He was ready to wrap this up anyway.

****
****

Across the lounge, Michelle was posted up in another VIP booth, laughing too loud with Jennifer and a local rap crew. Jennifer had come with Brick, all smiles and free drinks, already acted like she belonged.

"Girl, you lucky as hell sittin' up here with Stacks," Jennifer said, grinning like she won the lottery.

Michelle sucked her teeth and popped open her compact. "Lucky where? He been actin' like I don't even exist."

She checked her face anyway. Perfect. As usual. She snapped the mirror shut and tossed it into her purse.

Jennifer rolled her eyes. "Please. He noticed you."

"He better," Michelle said, smoothing her dress. "I ain't come out for vibes."

Michelle knew exactly what she brought to the table. Five nine. Big chest. Tiny waist. Ass that made men forget their birthdays. Men loved to look, but touching came with a price. Always had. She didn't give away samples.

She didn't even like Jennifer. Truth was, Jennifer was just a stepping stone. Loud mouth, hood connected, always knew who had money and where it was moving. And tonight, that connection landed Michelle right next to Stacks. Mission in progress.

Jennifer laughed at something off to the side as four women slid into the booth beside them, already drunk, already messy.

"Man, fuck him," one of them said loud as hell. "He hit and dipped and ain't leave me shit. Humph, he will never get this pussy again."

Another laughed. "Same. Dudes be broke and bold."

Michelle leaned toward Jennifer, lips barely moving. "Women don't got no shame no more."

Jennifer snorted.

One of the girls turned. "Excuse me? You talking 'bout us?"

Michelle smiled slow. "If the shoe fits."

The air shifted.

One of the women stood up, eyes locked on Michelle like she'd been waiting for this moment. "Oh, nah. I been lookin' for you."

Michelle's stomach dropped.

"You the bitch walking round here with my man."

She was suddenly way too close.

Michelle froze. Heart racing. Hands cold. She didn't fight. Never had to. This was not the plan. She was so scared she wanted to shit herself.

Jennifer thought the whole thing was funny. She leaned back, amused, sipping her drink like she was watching a show. She was sick of Michelle, anyway. This wasn't her problem.

"What you gon' do, bitch?" The girl snapped.

Before Michelle could answer, *pow*.

The room spun. Her face burned.

"And you want some, too?" The girl snapped at Jennifer.

Jennifer shook her head immediately and stood up. "Nah. I'm good."

She walked off without looking back.

Michelle tasted blood and panicked.

****
****

Across the lounge, Tremaine swallowed the rest of the Grey Goose in his cup and grimaced.

"Yeah," he muttered, already standing, "I'm done with this shit."

He headed toward Brick, jaw tight, eyes sharp.

The night had officially gone left.

"Yo, I'm out," Tremaine said, face tight as he stood.

Darius blinked at him. "It ain't even two a.m. yet. Where the girls at?"

Tremaine shook his head, already halfway turned. "I don't give a fuck. That broad Michelle? You can have her. Ain't nothin' in here for me."

He started toward the exit, the bass thumping behind him, when someone came running up fast enough to grab his attention.

"Stacks!"

Jennifer was breathless, eyes wide, panic all over her face. "Michelle's in trouble."

Tremaine stopped, turned slowly, and stared at her like she had completely lost her mind. He didn't get involved with drama or beef. He managed to stay in the street eighteen years with no problems, and he wasn't about to have one over no bitch.

"That ain't my problem," he said flat. "Take that shit to Brick."

He turned back around.

Jennifer grabbed his arm. Hard. "Please, help her."

He looked down at her hand, then up at her face. The fear wasn't fake. Whatever was happening wasn't cute club drama.

He exhaled through his nose. "Fuck."

He pivoted and walked straight back to Brick. "Come handle somethin' with me."

Brick didn't ask questions. He just nodded and followed. He'd known Tremaine since they were twelve. He knew when his friend said something, he meant it. Tremaine was known as Stacks on the street and was no one to be played with. He didn't hang with a lot of dudes or floss his money like most drug dealers. Tremaine was more business oriented and that's where many underestimated him. Brick was ready for whatever was to come.

They weaved through the crowd, Brick's hand instinctively brushing his waist, checking that his burner was still where it belonged. Old habits.

People started parting as they pushed forward.

Then they saw it.

A thick circle of bodies. Loud voices. Phones out. Energy wrong.

Brick glanced at Stacks. "Yeah," he muttered. "This already look stupid."

Tremaine's jaw tightened as he stepped toward the crowd.

Whatever was going on, it was about to stop.

Chapter Two

"What the fuck is goin' on?" Tremaine asked, already annoyed.

He stopped at the edge of the crowd, not eager to jump into whatever nonsense was popping off. Brick, on the other hand, moved like he'd been waiting for chaos all night.

"Of course you would," Tremaine muttered as Brick pushed straight through the bodies like Moses parted the Red Sea.

Tremaine turned to Jennifer. "What is *that* about?"

She shrugged; lips pursed. "Some chick said she was your girl and started beatin' on Michelle."

Tremaine laughed once—sharp and humorless. "Get the fuck outta here with that dumb shit."

Jennifer raised a brow.

"I don't got a girl. No wife. No main. No side," he said flat. "Everybody I deal with get treated the same. I make that clear."

He shook his head. "Chicks is outta control these days."

Still, curiosity pulled him forward. He needed to see which one of the many women he'd entertained had suddenly decided to claim ownership. That wasn't his vibe. Never had been. He let it be known from the jump that he was not going to be tied down.

He followed behind Brick and stopped short.

Michelle was on the floor.

Hair everywhere. Dress twisted. Getting stomped by a girl Tremaine knew all too well.

"Yo," he said, laughing under his breath. "You gotta be fuckin' kidding me."

Lisa.

Security was halfway in it, trying to break them apart, but Lisa was wildin', swinging like she had something to prove.

Brick was right in the middle, yelling at security, trying to separate bodies.

Tremaine shook his head, backing up.

Lisa had been cool before this. Grown. Calm. Or so he thought. But this? Fighting in the club?

Bird behavior. He had a reputation to maintain. Any woman he even considered to wife couldn't be on that fighting in the club shit.

He wasn't even embarrassed. Just tired of the dumb shit.

He leaned toward Brick. "This shit crazy. I'm gone."

Brick glanced back, nodded once. "Aight."

Tremaine didn't look back again. Tremaine was fed up with the type of women he was meeting. He exited the club and sighed.

Outside, the cool air hit him hard. He exhaled, long and heavy. "I can't wait to get my ass home."

He checked the time. 1:30 a.m.

Too drunk to drive. Too irritated to deal with anybody else.

He pulled out his phone and called his sister.

"Hello?"

The voice wasn't hers.

He frowned, checking the number. "Who is this? Where is my sister."

"This is Brielle," the woman said casually. "Ayesha not available right now. Is this Tremaine?"

Music thumped in the background. Definitely another party.

"Yeah," he said slowly, surprised to hear his government name being called. "Where y'all at?"

"Some club on Mercer Court."

Tremaine smirked despite himself.

Another night. Another mess.

And somehow, it felt like something was just getting started.

Tremaine froze when it hit him.

Same damn club.

He lifted the phone back to his ear. "Get my sister and come outside."

Click.

A few minutes later, Brielle stepped out into the night air.

Tremaine's eyes flicked up—and paused.

Damn. She is fine.

He caught himself immediately. Nah. Not like that. Never like that. Brielle had been around forever. Little sister status. Off limits, no matter what.

"I didn't know you was gonna be here," Brielle said, folding her arms. "She could've came with you."

The look on her face said she was already irritated.

"What's with the face?" Tremaine asked.

"I got schoolwork to finish. And clubs ain't my thing," she said flat. "I'm ready to go."

"Where Ayesha at?" He asked, scanning the door.

"She was right behind me."

Tremaine's chest tightened. He was trying to get the hell out before Michelle or Lisa stumbled outside looking for round two.

He pressed his keys into Brielle's hand. "Go sit in the car. Red Maserati, middle of the block. Lock the doors."

She nodded and walked off.

Tremaine turned and went right back inside.

The smell hit him first. Alcohol. Sweat. Regret.

He spotted his sister in the corner, bent over, throwing up like her life depended on it.

"Yo," he snapped, rushing over. "What the fuck are you doing here?"

She groaned. "Why you talkin' so loud?"

"Because you are embarrassing me," he muttered, wrapping an arm around her. "Come on."

She leaned into him, dead weight, and he dragged her toward

the exit.

Outside, the cool air barely helped.

They didn't get far before Michelle popped up outta nowhere.

"You leavin' with *this* drunk bitch?" She yelled.

Michelle looked crazy. Blood on her lip. Hair everywhere. Dress ripped like she went ten rounds with reality.

Tremaine didn't even stop walking. He wanted to get his sister out of the area. The stench of alcohol was coming from her clothes.

"Asshole!" Michelle screamed after him

He ignored her and kept walking to his car

Brielle jumped out quick to help.

"Damn, how y'all even get in there?" Tremaine asked, easing Ayesha into the backseat. "That club twenty-one and up."

Ayesha laughed weakly. "Your name rings bells."

That one hit him.

Hard.

Tremaine looked at his sister and became disgusted with himself. He realized that he was a bad influence in her life.

Eight months.

That's how long it had been since he'd seen her.

Their father was gone, and instead of him being a positive male influence for his twenty-year-old sister, he was helping to destroy her life by not watching over her like he should have.

He rubbed his face, jaw tight.

Yeah.

He had some shit to fix.

Tremaine didn't need a toxicology report to know something was wrong. Ayesha's pupils were blown wide, her skin slick with sweat, her body too restless for alcohol alone.

"What is she on?" He snapped at Brielle.

"I don't know," Brielle said, struggling to keep her voice steady as she buckled Ayesha into the back seat. "I don't drink. I don't do drugs. All I know is some dude kept buying her drinks. I told her to slow down. She wouldn't listen."

Tremaine reached to shut the door, but Ayesha shoved it back open and leaned forward just in time to vomit onto the concrete. The sound turned Brielle's stomach. She rushed to her side, gripping Ayesha's shoulders as her breathing went ragged and fast.

"Something's wrong!" Brielle screamed.

"We're taking her to the hospital. You drive," Tremaine said, already climbing into the back seat. Letting someone else drive his car went against everything he was. But his hands were shaking, his head spinning, and the last thing he needed was flashing lights and handcuffs. Not tonight. He was going to be in some deep shit with his mother when she got wind of this. Brielle raced to the driver's seat. She started the car and pulled out like a bat out of hell.

"Damn, slow down before you kill us," Tremaine barked as the car swerved through traffic.

Brielle didn't answer. Her knuckles were white on the steering wheel, eyes locked straight ahead.

"Forget it. Just get us there," he muttered, pulling Ayesha closer as her body trembled against his chest.

This was on him. All of it. Keri Should've checked on her sooner. Should've paid attention instead of being distracted by bullshit that didn't matter. He knew the life he lived bled into everyone around him, and now his baby sister was paying the price.

Ayesha let out a broken sob, her breathing uneven. Tremaine clenched his jaw, his heart pounding harder with every mile.

"Hold on, Ayesha," he whispered, guilt settling heavy in his gut. "I got you. I promise."

They made it to the hospital in ten minutes flat. Ayesha cried and moaned the entire ride, her body twisting like it was fighting itself. By the time they stopped, Brielle was trembling so hard she could barely open the door.

Tremaine didn't wait. He scooped his sister into his arms and ran, his chest tight, his mind already racing to the fallout. His mother was going to lose her mind.

Brielle locked the car and followed. She would be so hurt if something happened to her friend. She knew she shouldn't have agreed to go to the club tonight. All she could do now is pray she hadn't just watched her best friend slip too far away.

Chapter Three

Tremaine stormed up to the security guard. "My sister needs a doctor—now!"

The guard barely looked up. "What's wrong with her?" *This was an emergency room. They all needed doctors,* the guard thought.

Tremaine slammed his fist on the counter. "She's on something! Can't breathe right!"

The guard's eyes widened, finally moving. He went to get a nurse immediately.

A nurse appeared moments later. "Bring her into triage," she instructed.

Tremaine carried Ayesha in, laying her on the table. Her body shook violently.

"Sir, you need to step back," the nurse said with urgency in her voice. She hit the intercom and paged a doctor.

Within minutes, the room was filled with medical staff. Tremaine backed up toward the door, heart hammering. *If anything happens to her…*he thought, stomach twisting. He couldn't forgive himself.

He spotted Brielle in the waiting area. Relief hit him even

before he spoke.

"Is she okay?" Brielle asked, standing quickly.

"I don't know," Tremaine said, shaking his head. His chest tightened. He hadn't checked on his sister in months, too caught up in the streets, the money, the grind. And now this—this could kill her.

Brielle stepped forward and wrapped him in a hug. Tremaine stiffened for a second. He hated public displays of affection, but right now, he needed it.

"She's going to be okay," Brielle whispered. "She's a fighter."

Her words were the only thing keeping him steady. He let her hold him, drawing in the comfort. He just wanted her to hold him and not let go.

Brielle was extremely upset about the whole situation, but she couldn't go crazy in front of Tremaine. She could tell that he felt fucked up about it all. She practically grew up with Ayesha. If she didn't make it, Brielle didn't know what she would do. Brielle's tears fell freely now. She had no family of her own, but Ayesha was hers. They were sisters in every way that mattered.

Tremaine took her into his arms and tried to console her. Tremaine rubbed her back, feeling the weight of his guilt pressing down. He had to pull away when he noticed his body reacting. Now was not the time for that.

The door to Ayesha's room opened. A doctor stepped out; expression grim.

"Is my sister alright?" Tremaine demanded.

The doctor's voice was firm. "Your sister had a combination of alcohol and methylenedioxymethamphetamine in her system. Her blood alcohol was well above the legal limit, and she suffered a mild heart attack. She's lucky to be alive."

Tremaine's chest tightened further. Lucky. That word didn't cover it. He clenched his fists, guilt burning hotter than anything else. He should've been there. He *had* to be better.

"What is that?" Tremaine asked, his jaw tight.

"Your sister had traces of MDMA in her system," the doctor replied. "Also known as Molly. I see kids in the ER every day with complications from this recreational street drug. Popping Molly alone can do serious damage. Mix it with alcohol? The consequences can be deadly."

Tremaine's fists clenched. "Can I see her?"

"No. She's being admitted and will be tested to make sure there's no damage to her brain, lungs, or immune system. You should go home and come back when visiting hours start at 8 a.m. She should have a room by then." The doctor turned and walked away, leaving Tremaine burning with frustration.

He knew Molly. He didn't touch it himself—weed was his only vice—but he knew every drug in the streets. He'd been deep in that life once, climbing the ranks, moving up so he didn't have to get his hands dirty—but he still made sure things ran straight every day.

What the hell was she thinking?

Brielle came running up, panic written all over her face. "Your mom's on the phone. I don't know what to tell her."

Tremaine swallowed hard. He knew he had to tell his mother what happened to his sister. He would deal with the consequences later.

He took the phone. "Hey, ma."

"Brielle said she was with you. I haven't seen you in damn near eight months," his mother said, voice sharp.

"I know, ma…I'm sorry," Tremaine muttered, guilt rolling over him like a wave.

"Spit it out, boy. What's wrong?"

Tremaine's chest tightened. His mom always knew when something was wrong with one of her kids. Always.

"Ayesha is in the hospital. She took some drugs and mixed it with alcohol."

"What hospital? I'm on my way."

He told her where they were and heard the phone disconnect.

Tremaine rubbed his face, the weight of everything pressing down. Eight months away, streets pulling him one way, family another. And now this, his little sister on the edge because of choices he couldn't control.

Tremaine handed Brielle back the phone and stepped outside. He needed air. Anything to get away from the thought of his sister lying in that hospital bed. His mom would be here soon.

He stood there, lost in thought, until he sensed someone behind him. He hated that. Turning, he saw Brielle. He looked at her more closely. She'd been his sister's best friend since they were kids, but tonight...she was grown. For a second, his head spun. I'm bugging, he thought. Too much alcohol, too much stress—no way he could even think about her like that. He turned away. Relief washed over him when he saw his mother stepping out of a cab, eyes sharp and demanding.

"What the hell happened to my child?" She barked.

"I wasn't there," Tremaine began, voice tight. "By the time I got her out, she was sweating, breathing fast...it was bad." Tremaine tried to explain

Keri Williams listened, but her jaw tightened as she thought about kicking his ass. She had begged him for years to leave the streets behind, to settle down. She tried so hard to shelter her children from the streets, but it didn't work. Tremaine started selling drugs at twelve, and now this—her daughter lying in a hospital bed, all because of the life he led.

"When will these kids learn there's nothing out here for them?" She muttered, shaking her head.

"What are they going to do now? It's three in the morning. I know I can't do anything tonight," she added.

"The doctor said go home and come back at eight a.m.," Tremaine replied.

"No use standing around then. Let's go home." Keri waved

Brielle over and pulled her into a tight embrace. "It's okay. Everything's going to be okay," she whispered. Brielle, her eyes red from worry, melted into the hug. She took to Brielle because Brielle was what she wanted in a daughter. She went to school; she didn't drink or do drugs. She knew nothing about the streets and what they had to offer. Brielle's father recently passed away and it sent her over the edge to where she almost committed suicide. Keri took her into her home and helped her get back on track.

Tremaine watched them. His mother's love, strict but unshakable, hit him like a gut punch. All the ways he'd tested her, all the chaos he'd caused—he felt it all now, heavy and real.

Keri and Brielle stepped toward him.

"Are you coming back to the house with us?" Keri asked.

Tremaine nodded, drained in every way. "Yeah. I'm coming."

The three of them walked to his car in silence. Unspoken prayers hung between them. For Ayesha. For Brielle. For the night that had almost destroyed everything.

Chapter Four

The ride home was quiet. Everyone was lost in their own thoughts.

Tremaine's mind replayed the night over and over. What would he say to his sister tomorrow? He felt like a hypocrite. Telling her, "don't do drugs. Don't do what I do," and yet here she was, almost killed. He realized he had to get his shit together, take care of his family before it was too late.

Brielle's thoughts were with Ayesha. She blamed herself for not stopping her friend from drinking. Brielle had an older sister and brother who did horrible things to her as a kid. Her escape from reality was to run to Ayesha's house. She was welcomed with open arms every time. No one knew the extent of the pain her family caused her. She walked around with that pain every day. The recent death of her father had nearly broken her. Now, if Ayesha didn't make it, Brielle didn't know what she would do.

Keri was silent, lost in her own worry. She wasn't ready to deal with Tremaine tonight because she was too upset. She knew he wasn't directly responsible for Ayesha being in the hospital, but he was involved in a life that had left her daughter vulnerable. For eighteen years, all she could do was pray for him.

When they arrived home, Brielle cut the engine. Tremaine stayed in the car, wanting space. She tapped on the window. He opened the door and stepped out.

"You okay?" She asked softly, reading him like a book. She couldn't handle him falling apart because she was barely holding on herself.

He shook his head, tears suddenly falling. Brielle pulled him into her arms. He held on, letting the warmth sink in. Brielle was deeply in love with Tremaine and he didn't even know it. She has had her eyes on him since she was eleven. She knew back then that nineteen-year-old Tremaine was not interested. She was now twenty-two and he was thirty.

Tremaine felt comforted in Brielle's arms. He was starting to get a feeling that he never felt before. The person standing in front of him had definitely grown up. She was no longer the little girl that was always following him around. She was a grown woman doing her thing. He looked down at Brielle's 5'4 frame. She was small but thick in all the right places. Abruptly, Tremaine let her go. He couldn't believe the thoughts running through his head.

"I wanted to be alone," he admitted, "but I see you're not leaving my side."

Brielle smiled faintly. The alcohol was fading, and his stomach growled. "You hungry?" He asked, breaking the silence.

"A little. What did you have in mind?" She asked.

"Pancakes, bacon, eggs. Classic," he said, rubbing his stomach.

"I can make some," Brielle offered. "I'm going inside. You coming?" She turned and walked away.

"Hell, yeah, I'm coming," he muttered, locking the car and following her.

****

Inside, the smell of bacon hit him. *She don't waste no time,* he thought, heading upstairs to check on his mom and take a shower. He walked down the hall, took a deep breath, and knocked on his mom's door. He heard her shuffling around and then the door opened. Keri gestured for him to sit. She loved having him home. It made her feel better knowing he wasn't in the streets. The streets didn't love anyone, she knew that too well. Her street life was behind her, and she was upset that Tremaine chose to live an identical life.

"I wanted to talk to you," she said, placing a hand on his shoulder. "Baby Boy, it's about time you settle down. You're thirty. The streets aren't a place for you anymore. You haven't been hurt or arrested yet, but who's to say that it won't happen?"

"Mama, I hear you," he said, standing to embrace her. "I'm comfortable right now with my lifestyle. I've been feeling I want to settle down, but I haven't found the right woman yet."

"The right woman might be right in front of you," Keri said

softly, eyes locking on his, "but you're so busy chasing money and ass in the streets. Life is too short, Baby Boy," she said. You do know this is your fault, right?" Keri added, finger aimed straight at his chest.

Tremaine didn't flinch. He stood there. Jaw tight.

"Your father went to jail doing the same damn thing you're doing," she snapped. "And now my baby is laid up in a hospital bed with drugs and alcohol in her system."

Her voice cracked, then rose again.

"You happy now?"

He swallowed it. Let her get it out. He wasn't about to let her break him further.

"I apologized, ma," he said quietly. "What else you want me to do? I didn't know she was into drugs," he said and put his head down.

She laughed bitterly.

"Of course you didn't know because your ass never comes over to check on us. I only hear from you on holidays and birthdays."

That one landed.

"When are you gonna stop what you doing and get your life together?" She sobbed. "When are you gonna stop being selfish and put your family first? When are you gonna stop acting like your damn father?"

That did it. Tremaine had heard enough at the mention of his father.

Tremaine's face hardened. "I'm sorry, mama," he muttered, already backing toward the door.

He didn't wait for her response. He couldn't.

He needed out. He was feeling like shit and didn't want to stay in the house any longer. He needed to escape reality. He was going to go home, light a blunt, and hit the bed. The house felt heavy. His chest felt tighter than it had all night. He checked his Rolex. 4:00 a.m.

"Fuck it. I tried," he muttered.

Downstairs, the kitchen light was on. Brielle sat at the table, TV humming low, fork in hand. She looked up and smiled like the world hadn't just fallen apart.

"I made you a plate," she said sweetly, sliding it toward him.

Pancakes. Bacon. Eggs. Exactly what he asked for.

"I'm gonna head home," he said, rubbing his face.

Her smile faded. "Why? What happened?" She asked with concern.

Tremaine had never opened up to a woman before. He never felt the need to. Growing up, he only had one need for a woman but there was something different about Brielle. He couldn't put his finger on it. He wasn't going to ponder on it either. He was in enough shit as it was with his mother. He wasn't trying to be any kind of influence on Brielle as he was to his sister.

"Nothing," he lied. "I just wanna be alone," he said, shaking his head.

She tilted her head. "I know I didn't make this food for nothing," she said with an attitude. She hopped up and wrapped it in aluminum foil. "There you go," she said, pushing the plate toward him.

"Thanks," he said, already halfway to the door.

"How you getting home?" She asked, right behind him. "You're intoxicated."

"I said I'm good," he said, turning around to look at her.

She folded her arms. "The last time a Williams told me 'I'm good,' they ended up in a hospital. So, you got two choices. Cab. Or I drive," she said with her hands on her hips.

He laughed. "You serious?"

He reached for the door. "You are too funny. I'm good."

She jingled something behind him.

Keys.

He spun around. *Damn, this girl got me.* Too tired to fight, he gave in.

She smirked.

"Alright, you win," he sighed. "I ain't even going home now." He patted his stomach. "I'm gonna eat this and knock out."

He turned back toward the kitchen.

Brielle grabbed his hand.

"I was just trying to look out for you," she said softly. "I can't help that I love you." Once she said that, she knew things were going to be complicated. His back was to her when she said it. She hoped he didn't hear her but he turned around slowly to face her.

Silence.

His back stiffened. He thought he heard Brielle say she loved him. *I had a little bit too much to drink,* he thought.

He turned slowly. "What you say?"

She froze. Took a breath. "I love you."

He stared at her like she'd just slapped him.

"I gotta sit down for this," he muttered, dropping onto the couch. "I haven't slept in three days. I'm bugging."

She stood there; eyes locked on him. Calm. Certain. Her caramel skin was flawless. He shook his head to get the thoughts of her out of his head.

"So, you love me?" He asked, voice rough. "What you love me for? I ain't shit. My own mama don't even love me." Brielle was disturbed by what he was saying. She knew who he was and what he was doing. She knew how much of a whore he was in the streets. But she didn't care about any of that. She knew the real Tremaine—the man that had great potential but got lost somewhere down the line.

That hurt her. She could see it in his face—drunk honesty, raw and ugly.

She stepped closer.

"What happened to the guy who told me and Ayesha to stay in school?" She asked. "What happened to the guy who said he was gonna own a couple of businesses and get out the hood?"

She crouched in front of him.

"What happened to the man who told me: 'anything you wanna be, you can be'?"

Her voice softened.

"That man is still you, Tremaine. You just forgot him."

He looked at her then. Really looked. He wanted her to stop talking.

And for the first time that night, the streets didn't feel louder than the truth.

"Who you are now isn't you, and you know it," Brielle said softly but with fire in her eyes. "But you been doing it for so long, you just got comfortable."

Tremaine looked up at her. He wanted her to stop. Every word was true, and he hated how much it stung. What he was doing, his life in the game, affected everyone around him. And damn, he was tired.

Too far in to walk away. Too much at stake. He knew if he tried, someone would die, maybe him, maybe someone he loved. Staying meant survival. Leaving meant freedom with two hundred fifty million dollars in his pocket…if he lived long enough to spend it.

"You done?" He asked, voice sharp. He stood and drifted into the kitchen, running a hand through his hair. He felt so fucked up inside. For the first time, he had no map, no plan, no control.

Brielle watched him go. Her chest ached seeing him like this, knowing he could do so much more, be so much more if he just applied himself. She decided it was time to retreat. She needed sleep. She'd check on Ayesha in the morning and figure out her next move then. Walking toward the stairs, she paused and glanced back. Tremaine sat at the kitchen table, head down, lost in the shadows. She whispered a silent prayer for him and headed to her room.

Chapter Five

Tremaine woke to the clanging of pots and pans. His head throbbed like a drumline. He blinked a few times, trying to remember where he was. Then it hit him—his mother's house. He groaned. "What the fuck am I doing here?" Still in his clothes, he dragged himself to the kitchen.

"Well, good morning, hot mess," Keri said, setting a kettle on the stove. "Want some tea?"

"No. I want to know why I'm here," he replied, rubbing his temples.

Keri laughed. "What, don't want to be home with your mama anymore? No wonder I haven't seen you in eight months."

Brielle entered, avoiding his gaze, and kissed Keri on the cheek. "Good morning," she said softly.

"What time are we visiting Ayesha?" She asked, making his stomach twist.

Tremaine froze at the mention of his sister. Memories of alcohol and Molly blurred together like smoke.

"As soon as we clean up," Keri said. Then she turned to him. "Did the doctor tell you what drug she took?"

"Molly," he said.

"What the hell is that?" Keri said, pacing. "Kids today take anything to get a high. What happened to good old-fashioned weed?"

Brielle tilted her head, curious. She knew the streets but not the chemicals. And she wasn't sure if Tremaine was involved in that life anymore. "Excuse me," he muttered, stumbling toward the bathroom, barely making it to the toilet before vomiting everything up.

Damn, how much did I drink? He said to himself.

Weakness stole his strength, and he collapsed against the counter.

A knock startled him.

"Are you okay?" Brielle's voice called.

Opening the door, she bent down, sweat damp on his skin as she pressed a cold washcloth to his forehead and helped him upright.

"Can you make it to the couch?" She asked.

He nodded and together they shuffled out. Keri appeared from the kitchen and shook her head. *Brielle would make the perfect wife for my son,* she thought.

Brielle stayed close, wanting to ensure he was alright. "I'm staying with Tremaine," she told Keri.

"That's nice of you," Keri said.

Inside, she was silently grateful. Brielle had class—brains, ambition, and no street drama. The kind of woman she wanted around her son.

"Take care of my boy," Keri said. Brielle nodded, then returned to Tremaine's side.

The kitchen smelled like bacon and toast. Brielle busied herself, gathering water, Tylenol, and burnt toast—perfect hangover cures. Tremaine watched her, and a blush rose on her cheeks. She hoped he hadn't remembered her words from that morning.

"Here," she said, setting the tray down. "Perfect hangover cure."

Tremaine sniffed the tray like he was unimpressed. "You think you slick, huh? You remember what you were saying this morning?" He asked, locking eyes with her. "I'm giving you a minute to remember while I clean up."

"You need help?" She asked.

"You'd love that," he laughed. "Don't think you understand the type of dude I am."

"How do you know?" She challenged, hands on her hips.

"Hold that thought." He strode to the bathroom, the sound of running water following soon after.

Brielle's mind raced. She wanted Prince Charming, a fairytale man—but Tremaine was far from her fantasy. Thirty years old, thirty women deep, a player through and through. Still, the eight-year age gap didn't matter to her. He was her best friend's brother, but seeing him now…it was different.

When the shower shut off, Brielle froze, unsure of what he'd do or say next.

Tremaine emerged, towel wrapped around his waist, water dripping from his hair. He felt her gaze on him. *Damn… she's looking real right,* he thought. Normally, he had no conscience with women—but Brielle? She was untouchable.

He headed upstairs, leaving her staring after him, heart racing, and mind spinning with questions she wasn't ready to answer.

****
****

Tremaine's towel barely clung to his waist as he trudged upstairs. His mind was a storm—guilt, frustration, and a strange, unfamiliar pull toward Brielle. He hated that pull. He hated that he couldn't just think of her as his little sister's friend anymore.

In the quiet of his old room, seeing it just as he left it brought a small sense of satisfaction. He hid his money all over his mother's house; no valuables were left behind in his apartment. If anything happened to him, his sister and mother would be secure.

He grabbed his phone and noticed twenty missed calls. Most were from Michelle. Calls from his crew—Tracey, Darius, and Twin—also popped up. Twin had been his friend the longest. He saw a missed call from his mother and called her back.

"Hello?" She answered.

"Hey, mama, I'm sorry I missed your call. I was lying down."

"The doctor said Ayesha has alcohol poisoning and is severely dehydrated. She has to stay for a few days to be monitored."

Tremaine shook his head. "I'm sorry if you feel I caused any of this."

"It's not only your fault she's in here. She knows better. But I'm not sorry for the things I said to you this morning. Life is too short. Get your shit together and grow the hell up."

"I'm working on it. It's not overnight," he said.

"Anyway, do you feel better?"

"Yeah, I feel much better. I'm about to head out, but I'll be back…"

"Okay, love you, Baby Boy."

"Love you, too, mama."

After ending the call, he dialed Twin.

"What's good?" Twin answered immediately.

"You tell me, all y'all calling me, something must be wrong." Tremaine put the phone on speaker and leaned back on his bed, still wearing a black wife beater, blue jeans, and grey-and-black Jordans.

"Nah, Darius told me about what went down at the club last night."

"I don't remember half of that shit. I got fucked up."

"Damn, my dude. How did you get home? Darius said you left him."

"Brielle drove," Tremaine admitted. "Ayesha…she's in the hospital with alcohol poisoning, and she was popping Molly."

"Get the fuck out of here?!" Twin laughed nervously.

"I'm dead ass. My mama coming at me about it me. I'm going through it right now."

"You're not going through anything. Wait till you got a pregnant wife, then you can talk," Twin joked.

"What you doing today?" Tremaine asked, desperate to escape the house and Brielle's watchful eyes.

"I'm meeting Darius and Tracey at his house. That's probably why they were calling you."

"Alright, I'll meet you there. I'm heading out now."

After ending the call, Tremaine grabbed his wallet and keys, took a last glance around the room and made sure he had everything before he opened the door. Brielle appeared in the hallway in just a towel. He couldn't help but stare.

This girl is really playing with me, he thought, trying to push past her.

"Why don't you want me?" She asked, batting her eyes.

Tremaine towered over her 5'4 frame with his 6' frame. Her caramel skin glistened, her dark hair tossed in a bun, innocence mixed with undeniable allure. He knew he should say something, but the truth was he was struggling with the attraction, and he couldn't let himself act on it.

"I got to go," he muttered, attempting to move past her again, heart racing.

Brielle didn't budge. "You can't just run away, Tremaine. You got to face things," she said softly, but her tone carried weight.

He exhaled and looked at her, feeling the pull. He hated the guilt and the desire all at once. Brielle was everything he couldn't have right now—everything that reminded him there was more to life than the streets, drugs, and chaos.

He shook his head. "Not today," he whispered, pushing through the tension and stepping toward the door. He realized that running away wasn't going to be that simple—not with Brielle, not with his guilt, and certainly not with the life he was tangled up in. Brielle brushed up against him. "I love you, and I'm not letting you just walk away from me."

Tremaine took a step back. "I'm flattered that you feel that way, but I can't do anything with you."

"Why? Cause of your mama and Ayesha? I thought you were grown," she said, hands on her hips.

"I am grown, and that's why I'm not trying to holler back at you. So, if you'll excuse me, I got people to see," he replied with attitude.

"You know what? Forget everything I said earlier. You're such a bastard!" She screamed, running into Ayesha's room.

Tremaine felt the sting of guilt but knew he was doing the right thing. He followed her and knocked on the door. She opened it and walked away, upset and hurt. He stood in front of her, his presence filling the small room.

"Look, I'm sorry," he said.

"Whatever," she muttered, arms crossed.

"What is it you want from me?" He asked, gently taking her hand.

"I want you. I want your heart, body, and soul," she said. Tears formed in her eyes. The sincerity in her voice hit him.

"How long have you felt like this?" He asked, brushing her tears away.

"Eleven, long years," she whispered.

"You mean to tell me you've been in love with me since you were eleven?" He asked.

"Yes, but you never paid me any mind," she said, sobbing.

"I was nineteen when you were eleven. I wasn't thinking about your young ass," he said.

"And I guess you're still not eleven years later," she shot back, looking up at him.

"You just don't know how to stop, do you?" He asked, struggling with the temptation.

"Stop what? Being honest? I thought men liked it when a girl kept it real," she said, eyes locked on his.

"I appreciate your realness but now is not the time for us to start anything," he said firmly.

"Who has to know?" She asked, walking toward him, rubbing against his chest. "You know you want me."

If only she knew, he thought, shaking his head. "Tell me something—are you just trying to fuck, or do you want something real?" His question was direct. He asked every woman this; their answer determined if he gave them the time of day.

"I don't just want to fuck you. I want all of you," she said.

Her words stirred something inside him. On any other day, he might have run, but he kept hearing his mother's voice, telling him to settle down. Yet, he also didn't want her nagging about his lifestyle. He also felt a like he was missing something in life. Something nice, sweet and calming to balance the chaos in his life. . Brielle had put him in a tight spot. He had loose ends to tie up before he could even consider a relationship with anyone.

"I'm feeling everything you're saying, but right now is not the time for me to have a relationship," he said.

Brielle looked like he'd just crushed her world. He couldn't stand seeing her hurt, so he quietly walked out, heart heavy, and headed to his car.

"Damn," he muttered, shaking his head as he started the engine and drove toward Darius's house, trying to push away thoughts of Brielle from his mind, though he knew he would fail.

Chapter Six

Tremaine grabbed his phone and called Darius. He needed to get his mind off Brielle and everything that had happened over the past few days.

"Yo, you good?" Darius asked.

"I'm good. I'll be there in a few. What y'all doing?"

"Drinking, smoking, and listening to music."

"That's what I'm talking about. We don't get to chill like we used to."

"Man, we all here waiting on your slow ass."

"Alright, I'm turning the corner now," Tremaine said, hanging up.

Pulling up to Darius's house, he saw two cars in the driveway and one in front. Being in the streets for so long had made him hyper-aware of his surroundings. He got out, checked the perimeter, walked up the steps, and knocked on the door.

Tracey answered, her Coca-Cola shaped body and blonde bob catching his attention for a second before he reminded himself that she was like a sister to him.

"What's up, Mr. Man?" She exclaimed, hugging him.

"I came to chill and get chocolate wasted!" He said, cracking a smile.

Inside, the boys lounged on the couch, smoke swirled through the air. Tremaine inhaled deeply, letting it take the edge off.

"What y'all smoking on? That shit smell good as hell," he said.

Darius threw a pound of weed onto the coffee table. "This is that Blue Velvet," he said.

"I don't give a fuck what it is. This shit right here is on point," Twin said, eyes already drooping from the high.

Tracey sat next to Darius, and Tremaine caught a small, fleeting look between them. He kept it in the back of his mind; he didn't need drama. Their crew ran clean—no unnecessary complications—and he intended to keep it that way until his reign was over.

Tremaine sat across from Twin and rolled a blunt, the foursome passed it back and forth. Darius was the true pothead, puffing away like it was a full-time job.

Twin glanced at his watch. "Damn, it's late. I gotta head out. Got to get up early to take Marie to the doctor. Any day now," he said, referring to the birth of his daughter.

"Alright homie. Get home safe. Call or text when you get there," Tremaine said, giving him a hug.

Darius was still puffing, chuckling, "Peace out my dude."

Tracey shook her head. "I thought y'all were going to have some bitches here."

Darius laughed. "Why you ain't say nothing? I thought this was just chill time. I can have some girls here in ten minutes."

"Make it happen, captain. And please, no ratchet ass loud bitches," Tracey shot back.

Tremaine let out a low chuckle, shaking his head. "Man…this crew stay doing the most."

Darius pointed between them. "Aight, say less." He turned and disappeared into the kitchen, already dialing his phone.

The second he was out of sight, the room shifted.

Tracey leaned back slow, eyes sliding over to Tremaine like she'd been waiting on this exact moment.

"You real quiet tonight," she said, voice smooth but messy underneath.

"I'm always quiet," Tremaine replied, but his shoulders had gone stiff.

Tracey hummed like she wasn't buying it. She leaned forward, elbows on her knees. "Nah…this that different quiet. This that 'I already know what's coming' quiet."

Tremaine finally looked at her, eyes narrowed. "You bored or you just fishing tonight?"

A slow smile spread across Tracey's face. "Maybe both."

From the kitchen, Darius's voice rang out, "Y'all better not be in there plotting."

Tracey didn't even look away from Tremaine. "Boy, hurry up!" She called back, then dropped her voice again. "I'm just saying...every time certain company show up, you get real...interesting."

Tremaine's jaw flexed. "You talk too much."

"But I don't talk wrong," she shot back quick.

Before he could answer, footsteps came from the kitchen.

Darius stepped back into the room like he was bringing the party with him. A few seconds later, he returned with four females.

The air shifted instantly.

Slowly...Tracey leaned back, folding her arms, that knowing smile creeping across her face.

"Oh yeah," she murmured under her breath, "...this about to get real interesting."

Tremaine watched as they walked into the house. One of them caught his eye immediately. She was about 5′6″ with flaming red hair pulled into a ponytail. Her caramel skin was flawless, light brown eyes framed by glasses, and she had curves that left an impression. Tremaine needed this distraction to get Brielle off his mind.

"Don't be shy, ladies. This is my man Stacks. He won't bite," Darius said, taking a seat on the couch.

The women joined him, and the redhead sat next to Tremaine. His pulse quickened instantly. "What's your name?" He asked.

"Unique," she replied, turning to him.

"That's a pretty name," Tremaine said, taking her hand lightly.

While he and Unique talked, her friends and Darius smoked and laughed in the background. Tremaine felt the tension in his chest ease slightly. He was ready to leave with her.

"I'm about to get up out of here. You got a number I can reach you at?" He asked.

"You're bold," she said with a playful smile, pulling out her phone. "I'll take your number."

Tremaine gave it to her. "I'm out, man," he said to Darius.

He said his goodbyes to the others and walked out. By the time he reached his car, his phone buzzed with a text from Unique: *I'm coming right behind you.*

He smiled and slid into the driver's seat just as she approached.

"What you trying to do?" She asked, her voice low and teasing.

"Whatever you're trying to do," he replied, matching her tone.

Unique, like the others he'd dealt with, knew who he was. Some played hard to get—but he knew it wouldn't take long.

"Let's go for a ride," she said.

Tremaine opened the door, and she got in. Hours later, back in a hotel room, he laughed quietly to himself. Mission accomplished.

Chapter Seven

After being with Unique that one time, she became attached. Tremaine continued to mess with her because she had a mean head game like no other he'd been with. But after two months of her questioning him about his whereabouts, he stopped talking to her. She was mad and kept sending him nasty texts. He didn't care—she knew the rules.

Tremaine hadn't been back to his mother's house since the day he left for Darius's. His mother informed him that Ayesha was in a rehab facility. She wanted him to come over, but he refused. He didn't want to see Brielle—though, truth be told, she was on his mind more than he cared to admit. Out of sight wasn't working; the longer he stayed away, the more he thought about her.

Tremaine had been considering leaving the game behind. He was getting older and wanted a family of his own. He started investing his money into property and stocks, knowing he couldn't stay in the drug game forever. He decided to stop by his mom's house to get some money, hoping she wasn't home so he could keep it quick and simple.

Turning the key in the door, it appeared no one was home. He ran upstairs to his room and didn't bother closing the door. He pulled out two shoeboxes and started counting money.

"What are you doing here?" Brielle's voice startled him.

Caught off guard, Tremaine looked at her. "I'm minding my business," he replied, returning to the money.

"You are such an asshole," she shouted, slamming the door.

Tremaine finished counting, took what he wanted, and replaced the boxes. He was about to leave, but something told him to check on Brielle. For him to care about a female's feelings was rare, so for him to actually go see if she was ok was a big step.

He knocked. She opened the door, her eyes red from crying. He pulled her into his arms. She snuggled up to him, and for a moment, he ignored the rules he usually followed.

"You want to take a ride?" He asked.

She nodded.

He took her hand, and they left the house. He opened the car door for her, and she buckled up.

"You hungry?" He asked, craving seafood.

"A little. What do you have in mind?" She asked shyly.

"Crab nachos are banging."

"I've never had that before, but I'll try it," she said.

Changing the subject, he asked, "So, what are you going to school for?"

"I'm getting a bachelor's in political science. I want to be a lawyer."

"That's impressive. I need a good lawyer in my life," he said, smiling.

Brielle blushed. "Thank you."

Tremaine thought about Ayesha. "Your friend needs to get her life together."

"I can't believe she's in rehab," Brielle said, concern etched on her face.

"Those hard drugs will do it to you," he replied.

She buried her face in her hands. "How could this have happened?"

"Don't worry about Ayesha. She'll figure it out, just like I have to. Now back to you—how long until you get your degree?"

"Two semesters, if I can come up with the money to pay for classes," she said. Cuts in financial aid meant she had to either pay out of pocket or take loans, both difficult options.

"You'll get it," he said firmly. "I'm going to give it to you."

Brielle blinked, clearly thrown. "Really? I…I don't know what to say. Thank you." Her voice softened at the end, like the words didn't fully capture what she was feeling.

Tremaine kept his eyes on the road. "You ain't gotta thank me like that."

She shifted in her seat, fingers fidgeting in her lap. "It's just…I'm not used to people stepping in for me."

That made him glance over.

"And that's supposed to be a good thing?" He asked quietly.

Brielle hesitated. "It's just how I learned to survive."

The honesty in her voice sat heavy in the car.

Tremaine exhaled slowly through his nose. "Ain't everything gotta be survival mode all the time, Brielle."

She gave a small, tired smile that didn't quite reach her eyes. "Easy for you to say."

Silence stretched between them, not awkward—just full.

After a moment, she spoke again, softer now. "I just don't want things getting…weird between us."

His hands tightened slightly on the wheel. "Helping you ain't weird."

"It can be," she said gently. "Money changes stuff. Expectations sneak in whether people mean for them to or not."

That made him look at her fully this time.

"You think I move like that?" He asked, voice low.

Brielle quickly shook her head. "No. That's not what I'm saying." She paused, choosing her words carefully. "I just…I've learned to be careful when somebody starts doing too much for me."

Something in his expression shifted—not anger, not exactly.

Something quieter.

"Maybe," he said after a beat, "you so used to being let down, you don't know what to do when somebody actually got you."

The words hit.

Brielle looked away fast, blinking like she needed a second to steady herself.

"That's not fair," she murmured.

Tremaine's voice softened just a notch. "Ain't trying to be."

Another quiet moment passed.

Then Brielle spoke, barely above a whisper. "I do appreciate it… more than you probably think."

His grip on the wheel eased.

"Good," he said quietly. "'Cause I meant it." he added, pulling into the parking lot.

And for the first time since the conversation started, the space between them didn't feel so guarded…just complicated in a way neither of them was ready to name.

****

Tremaine and Brielle were seated in a cozy corner of Joe's Crab Shack, away from the crowd. Tremaine ordered the crab nachos as an appetizer, and Brielle couldn't stop smiling, still in disbelief that she was actually here with him.

"What are you smiling about?" He asked, leaning back in his chair.

"Nothing…just that I can't believe I'm actually here," she said, glancing around nervously.

Tremaine chuckled. "You're supposed to be excited, not nervous."

They dug into the crab nachos, the mix of cheese, crab meat, and spices making them both reach for more. Brielle picked at the plate shyly, trying not to seem greedy, while Tremaine practically attacked his half.

The quiet rode between them for a minute before Tremaine spoke again.

"So, what you be doing when you not in school?" He asked, voice easy.

Brielle glanced over at him, lips curving just a little. "Nothing too exciting. School, work, home. I'm real predictable."

Tremaine let out a soft chuckle. "Yeah…I don't believe that."

"Oh?" She said, turning toward him slightly. "And what makes you so sure?"

. "You don't give predictable energy."he said

Brielle smirked and folded her arms loosely. "You reading energy now?"

"I read what people show me," he replied smoothly.

She studied him for a second, like she was trying to figure out if he was serious or just slick with it.

"You always this confident?" She asked.

"Only when I know I'm right," Tremaine said without missing a beat.

That pulled a quiet laugh out of her.

"Mmm," Brielle hummed, taking a slow sip of her soda. "You real sure of yourself."

His mouth tilted slightly. "Confidence make you nervous?"

She met his eyes then, holding his gaze just long enough to make the moment stretch.

"...Not nervous," she said softly. "Just paying attention."

Something in Tremaine's expression shifted, just a fraction.

"Good," he said low. "'Cause I'd hate to think you wasn't."

Brielle shook her head, but the small smile playing on her lips gave her away.

"You talk real smooth," she murmured.

Tremaine leaned back slightly in his seat, voice calm but loaded.

"Only when the company worth it."

That did it.

Brielle looked out the window quick, but the faint color rising in her cheeks didn't miss him.

And Tremaine?

Yeah... he caught every second of it.

Brielle laughed at how messy he was with the cheesy sauce on his fingers, and he teased her about being a "clean freak." The small talk made the tension between them feel lighter, the conversation flowing easier than either expected.

Once they finished eating, Tremaine stood and held out his hand. "Ready to roll?"

Brielle nodded, excitement and nerves mixing together.

He led her back to the car, opened her door, and helped her

in. The drive to his house was quiet at first, just the hum of the engine and the occasional turn of the radio dial. Brielle watched the neighborhoods pass by, trying to take in the sights while keeping her hands in her lap.

"Your place isn't too far," she said finally.

"You're about to see it," he said with a grin, glancing at her. "Hope it impresses you."

When they pulled up, Brielle stared. "Whose house is this?"

"Mine," he said, opening the door for her. "You like it?"

"It's beautiful," she said softly.

Inside, the baby blue and chocolate brown theme was warm and inviting. Artwork decorated the walls, the living room filled with gadgets, flat screens, and subtle touches of luxury. Brielle knew Tremaine hadn't decorated it himself—it had a professional, curated feel—but she was impressed.

"This is nice," she commented, stepping further inside.

"You like it?" He asked, a small smirk on his face.

"Yep. Who decorated this place?" She asked, sarcasm lacing her tone.

"I did." he said. Everything here, I earned it."

Brielle looked around again, real slow this time—the big couch, the glass table, the oversized painting on the wall

"You did all this yourself?" she asked, one eyebrow lifting.

"Yeah," he said, a little proud. "Why?"

She folded her arms, trying not to smile. "I mean… it's nice.

Real nice."

He narrowed his eyes. "But?"

"But," she said, shrugging, "I didn't know you had such... *expensive taste.*"

"Meaning?"Brielle nodded, taking it all in. "Well, you definitely earned it."

She had only stepped into the living room, and even that felt unreal. If this was just the front of it, she could only imagine what the rest looked like.

"I'm about to smoke a fat ass blunt and chill," Tremaine said casually. "Make yourself at home."

He headed toward his bedroom, and after a brief hesitation, Brielle followed.

The moment he stepped inside, he kicked off his sneakers and peeled his shirt over his head. By the time he reached the dresser, he was down to his boxers, moving with the kind of confidence that came from never doubting himself. He disappeared into the closet.

"You good, baby?" He called out.

"I'm okay," she said softly, standing near the door.

He stepped back out, watching her like he was trying to figure her out. "So, you really want to be my girl? My wifey? My boo?" He asked with a half-smile.

"Yes. I do," she said without flinching. "The one and only."

He chuckled under his breath. "I don't know about all that."

Brielle's mind drifted somewhere dangerous. She wanted him badly, felt it in her chest, in her thighs, in the way her pulse jumped every time he looked at her. But she stayed still. She didn't want to rush this. Didn't want to be another woman who gave him her body and lost his attention the next day.

"Come here," Tremaine said, stepping toward her.

She didn't move.

That surprised him.

He wasn't used to women hesitating. Most of them were aggressive, needy, loud. Brielle wasn't any of that. There was something steady about her, something real. And that scared him more than it should have.

Money and the streets were all he knew. They raised him. Shaped him. His father had been locked up since Tremaine was sixteen, taken down by someone close, someone trusted. Twenty-five years for selling cocaine. Justice had come later. Quietly. Violently. After that, Tremaine stopped feeling much of anything.

Until now.

He pulled her into his arms anyway.

"Why do you want to be with me?" He asked, searching her brown eyes.

Up close, she was even more beautiful. Caramel skin. Soft. Untouched by the hardness she carried.

"I don't," she said, sucking her teeth and looking away.

He sighed, feeling something unfamiliar twist in his chest. He could see the hurt she was trying to hide, and for the first time, it mattered.

"I need to tell you something."

He crossed the room and grabbed a framed photo from the bookshelf. When he turned back, Brielle recognized the face immediately.

"I remember your father," she said carefully. "What happened to him?"

"He's locked up since I was seventeen. Serving twenty-five years," Tremaine said flatly. "My moms didn't want my sister to know, so she told her he walked out on us. Truth is, a family friend snitched. Feds raided everything. A year later, I found out who did it…and I handled it."

Her breath caught, but she didn't interrupt.

"That was the first time I ever pulled a trigger," he continued. "I learned quick not to trust nobody. Been hustling since I was twelve. Weed first. Then crystal. I don't keep friends. I don't let people get close. I don't know how."

He studied her face, trying to read it. "What you thinking?"

She swallowed hard. "I'm trying to process all of that."

Then she lifted her eyes to his. "But let me tell you something. I'm not here to judge you or hurt you. I know the streets. They took my mother from me. She chose crack over her kids. Chose it over protecting me."

Her voice trembled but didn't break.

"My father saved me from her just to throw me away later. Said I reminded him too much of her. My aunt let me stay until I turned eighteen, then I was back outside again. So, I survived however I could. Dancing. Selling myself. Stealing. Whatever kept me alive."

Tears finally fell.

"I know what it feels like not to trust anyone," she whispered. "The only people I feel safe with is your family."

She broke then, sobbing into his chest.

Tremaine wrapped his arms around her and held her tight. "Damn…I didn't know you were living like that."

He kissed her forehead. "It's gonna be okay. I got you."

She pulled back just enough to look at him. "Do you mean that?"

His face was serious now. No games. No smiles.

"I'm gonna take care of you, baby girl," he said. "I'm not letting nobody hurt you again. I just need a few days to get my shit together."

For the first time in a long time, he meant every word.

Brielle leaned in and pressed her lips to his, catching him off guard. Sparks shot through him the moment their mouths met. Heat pooled low in his body, reminding him just how badly he wanted her. But he knew it wasn't the right time. Reluctantly, he pulled back slightly, letting her linger there, and walked into his closet to grab his supplies for a blunt.

When he reemerged, Brielle stood in the doorway like a scared little girl. He froze for a second, unsure what to say or do before he sat on his bed. Silence felt heavier than usual. Tremaine hated when someone just stood there doing nothing—it made him tense.

"Brielle, come here," he finally said, patting the space next to him on the bed.

Slowly, she made her way over and sat down. He reached out and cupped her face in his hands. "I'm feeling you. You're smart, got your head on straight. A dude like me…I need someone like you in my corner. You don't have to be afraid. I'm not gonna hurt you."

"I don't want my heart broken again," she admitted softly, her eyes glistening.

"That's not what I'm here for," he said, brushing a thumb across her cheek.

He lit the blunt, inhaled deeply, and leaned back against the headboard. Usually, smoking with a girl didn't faze him, but doing it with Brielle stirred something he couldn't quite name.

"It's funny…I've known you for so long and I don't really know anything about you," he said.

"What do you want to know?" She asked cautiously, hoping he wouldn't pry into her family drama.

"Tell me about your family. Do you have siblings? Shit, you were at my mom's house so much, I figured you practically lived there."

Brielle hesitated. "I told you a little about my mom already. I have a sister and a brother—they're older than me. My father passed a few months ago...and I don't know what happened to my mom. I moved in with my aunt when I was fifteen." She lowered her gaze, and he noticed the shadows of sadness under her eyes.

"I'm sorry to hear about your father," he said quietly.

"I'm okay. I just...miss him a lot," she sighed, her voice catching.

Tremaine didn't push further. Instead, he pulled her closer, letting the silence and the smoke fill the space between them, a quiet understanding forming that neither needed to rush.

Tremaine laid back down and sighed. He was digging this woman in front of him. His mind was saying not to fuck with her, but he felt something in his heart telling him to go for it. He didn't know what love felt like either. The majority of the women he was with were with him for his money or a drug connection. He wanted to be loved for him, and it seemed like that was what Brielle was trying to do.

She laid back and placed her head on his chest. She had never experienced love before. At one point in time, she thought she did, but he had only been in love with the sex not her. She was dying to know what real love felt like.

The couple lay in silence. Tremaine blew his blunt down, and Brielle listened to his heartbeat. She had waited for this moment for years, but now that it was finally happening, she didn't know how to respond.

Tremaine started rubbing her dark brown hair. She looked up at him. He kissed her. She kissed him back. He pulled her up on top of him.

"I wouldn't mind taking it there with you, but you do know being with me comes with consequences." he said looking into her eyes. "A lot of adjustments will have to be made. I don't have a lot of free time to give to you. All that other stuff, I got you, but time is something I can't do right now."

"Why don't you just give it up?" She asked with a serious look on her face. Tremaine looked at her like she was crazy. He was comfortable and wasn't ready to deal with the consequences of leaving the game.

"Eventually I will, but I can't just leave like that. There is too much at stake."

"Even if the right woman came along for you. Don't you want a family?" She asked.

Tremaine was beginning to feel empty inside lately. He was tired of coming home to an empty house. He was tired of sleeping with random women. He just wanted someone to have his back. Someone to share his money and house with.

"Yea, I do."

"So, why don't you work on that. You are not getting any younger," she said kissing his lips.

"Do you have condoms?" She asked.

Tremaine looked at her like she was crazy. "Of course, I have condoms. Why you ask?"

"Cause I want to make love to you," Brielle said.

Tremaine couldn't believe the words coming out of this girl's mouth. She just never failed to amaze him. He was high as hell and not in the right state of mind. She was asking for it, so he was going to give her the business.

He got up from the bed and returned with a six-pack of Magnum condoms. Brielle wasn't impressed. She found that most dudes who used Magnums couldn't fill it properly. She just hoped he wasn't a "mini me." That would be such a shame.

She took the pack from him and seductively said, "show me what you're working with."

Tremaine didn't know how to take Brielle. He was used to getting straight to business—fuck them and then put them out. But he knew that wasn't happening with the woman he had in front of him. He never woke up to a woman before, never talked to a woman during sex, or even held a woman afterwards. Yet, he wanted to do all of that with Brielle.

"Fuck it. I'm not shy," he said and took his boxers off.

Brielle gasped at the ten inches of chocolate in her face. Her panties instantly became wet as she reached for Tremaine's hardened penis. Brielle was ready to be with the man that she loved.

Tremaine pushed her back on the bed. After removing her

jeans, he positioned himself on top of her and began kissing her. Brielle moaned and squirmed underneath him. She wanted him, and he was teasing her.

Brielle pushed him off her and got up to remove her clothes, revealing her naked body. Tremaine took in the sight of her 36C breasts and flat stomach. Sitting up, he reached out for her, but she moved away to turn off the lights. When she came back to him, she hugged him tightly. They were both nervous. Neither wanted the other to know they had never had sex with love involved.

Too late to turn back, Brielle thought.

She lay back as Tremaine kissed her lips delicately. Next, he moved down to her breasts, she stiffened up. Tremaine felt her tensing up. To try to get her to relax, he caressed her face.

"We don't have to do this."

"I want to," she whispered.

Tremaine went back to her breasts. When he placed his mouth on her nipple, she moaned. Using his tongue, he made circles around her areola. He moved down lower, but when he got to Brielle's love canal, he stopped. He had never given a female oral sex. Although he didn't have a clue what he was doing, he wasn't going to let her know that. So, he placed his mouth over her clitoris and started sucking. Brielle tried to move away, but he firmly held her in place. She grabbed the back of his head and moaned his name in ecstasy. The louder she moaned, the harder he sucked.

"Baby, please stop," she whispered.

Tremaine raised himself up to face her. She had a condom in her hand.

"I want to feel you inside of me."

He took the condom from her, put it on, and laid her back. She started kissing him. Her body was warm, and she was extremely wet. He didn't have a problem sliding inside of her. Once inside, Tremaine couldn't control himself. She felt so good. He buried himself deep inside her. She screamed out in pleasure. She thrust her hips to match his movements.

"I love you, Tremaine," she cried.

"I love you, too," he moaned back.

Chapter Eight

They held each other tight, bodies moving to a rhythm that belonged only to them. When it was over, Tremaine collapsed against Brielle, her quiet sobs soaking in his chest.

"What's wrong?" He asked, lifting himself enough to see her face.

"I don't want this to be just sex with you," she said, her voice cracking.

He didn't hesitate. "It's not. You mean more to me than that. I told just you I love you, and I meant it. I've never said that to any woman besides my mom and my sister."

She curled into him, her head resting against his chest.

"Damn," Tremaine muttered. "What kind of dudes you been dealing with?"

Brielle sighed. "The kind that only wanted one thing."

"Well, I'm not them. We didn't even have to do this for me to be here." He kissed her forehead. Brielle shifted closer, letting her head rest on Tremaine's chest. His heartbeat was steady under her ear, and she could smell his cologne mixed with the faint city air drifting through the cracked window.

"I could stay like this forever," he said, voice low, warm.

"You're saying that because you're comfortable, or because you like me," she teased, lifting her head just enough to smirk at him.

He laughed, brushing a strand of hair behind her ear, his fingers lingering against her cheek. "Both. You're intoxicating. Soft. And you know exactly how to make me want more."

"Good. That's the plan," she said, nudging him with her shoulder, letting the corner of her mouth twitch in a grin.

He leaned down, lips brushing the top of her head, and whispered, "I'm serious though. I want to know all of you. Even the quiet, weird parts you don't show anyone."

"I thought you were joking," she said, her lips curving up in a half-smile, half-laugh. "I'm not just the fun, easy parts. I have nights like this, too. Nights when I'm complicated, messy, stubborn."

"I like complicated," he said. His fingers traced lazy patterns along her arm. "Makes the easy parts sweeter."

She laughed softly, tilting her head against his chest. "Is that your excuse for being irresistible?"

"Maybe," he said, pressing a kiss to her temple. "Or maybe I'm just honest. I will always stay. I hope you'll let me."

"I already have," she said, voice soft, heart quickening. "I think I always have."

They lay there, listening to the city hum through the window.

Somewhere down the block, music spilled from a neighbor's house. Car tires squeaked. A dog barked. The world outside moved on around them, but in this little patch of blankets and low light, it was just them.

"You make the city feel smaller," he murmured, wrapping his arm over her shoulder. "Like it's ours for tonight."

"Then let's pretend it is," she said, tightening her hold on his hand. "Right now, this…us…is enough."

He pressed a soft kiss to her forehead, and she laughed into his chest, teasing, "Don't get all sentimental on me."

"I already am," he said, grinning against her hair. "But it suits me. Just like you."

Brielle rolled her eyes but smiled anyway, tugging the blankets up and settling closer, letting the warmth between them linger. The soft glow of the city through the window cast gentle shadows across the room.

Tremaine's fingers drifted into her hair. She yawned, stretching one arm across his chest.

"Sleepy?" He asked quietly.

"Yeah," she whispered. "But I don't want to move."

"Then don't," he said, pulling her even closer. "We'll stay like this. I've got you."

Brielle closed her eyes, letting the steady rhythm of his heartbeat carry her away.

Tremaine shifted slightly, resting his head against hers. "Good night, Brielle," he murmured.

"Goodnight, Tremaine," she replied softly, her hand clutching his.

Finally, they drifted into sleep, tangled together, perfectly at peace in each other's arms.

Chapter Nine

Tremaine woke up to his phone buzzing on the dresser. "Damn…what time is it?" He blinked hard and grabbed the phone. His mom.

"Yeah, ma."

"Well, good morning to you, too," she said. "I haven't heard from you in a while."

He sat up and rubbed his face. He wasn't in the mood for a lecture this early. "I've been busy getting my stuff together, like you told me to."

"Oh, really? So should I be expecting a daughter in law and some grandbabies soon?"

He nearly choked. "Let's not get ahead of ourselves."

"Have you seen Brielle? She wasn't here when I got home from work."

"No, I haven't seen her," he answered. He couldn't let his mother know Brielle was with him for both of their sakes.

"Ayesha's coming home next week. I'm throwing her a small welcome home party."

"That's cool."

"I know it's early. I'll let you go."

When the call ended, Tremaine checked the time. Nine a.m. Way too early for him. He usually didn't move before twelve. Brielle wasn't in the room, so he decided to shower.

Afterward, he felt human again. He checked himself in the mirror and smirked.

"Still got it."

He threw on dark jeans, a black tee, and his grey and black Jordans. Sneakers were his thing. Over two hundred pairs and counting. Once he was satisfied with his look, he headed downstairs.

He wasn't looking for Brielle. But when he reached the living room, he heard movement in the kitchen. He paused, then walked in.

Brielle was cooking.

She had on one of his wife beaters and nothing else. His jaw tightened.

"You hungry?" She asked casually.

"Nah," he said, voice rough, eyes glued to her. "I'm about to blow one."

She laughed. The sound playful. "Always that dramatic?"

"Not usually," he said, stepping closer. "But you…you got me messed up."

"You mean scared," she said, smirk teasing, eyes locking on his. "Scared of me?"

"Yeah," he admitted, rubbing the back of his neck. "And scared of dragging you into my world. Streets, drama…it's not fair to you."

Brielle set the spatula down, crossing her arms. "Tremaine, I know your world isn't perfect. But I'm not scared of you. I'm scared of losing you…but not of you."

He swallowed hard while looking at her, feeling conflicted. "That's just it. I don't know if I can be the guy you need. The guy you deserve. I can't promise tomorrow."

"Then promise what you can," she said softly, stepping closer. "Right now. Not your streets. Not your past. Just us."

He hesitated, then pressed a hand to her cheek. "Brielle…I love you. But I can't ignore the risk. I can't ignore what I am."

She let out a shaky laugh.

"But I mean it. I don't want you thinking you're only here for sex. You mean more than that to me."

Her eyes glistened as she reached for his hand. "I know. And I love you for it. But it scares me too. I can't…I can't have you the way I want. Not fully."

He pulled her into a hug, holding her tight, rubbing her back. "I know," he whispered. "But we'll figure it out. One step at a time."

They moved back to the counter, sitting across from each other with plates of food she had prepared. They ate in silence at first, the sizzling sounds from the pan lingering in the background.

Tremaine watched her with a soft intensity, and Brielle caught his gaze.

"So," she said finally, twirling her fork. "If we're talking next steps…what does that even look like?"

He leaned back, running a hand through his hair. "I want us. I want kids. A family. Marriage…all of that. But it can't happen overnight. I've got too much going on. Too many things I need to fix first."

"Kids?" She asked, eyebrow raised. "You're serious?"

"Yeah," he said, smiling. I want that someday. But right now…we work through us first."

She smiled back, leaning across the counter to kiss his cheek. "Okay. Then we start with us."

****
****

Later, they moved to the bedroom. Clothes fell away, laughs and whispers mixed with the city sounds outside. Hands traced skin, mouths found each other, and the world beyond those walls didn't exist. Every kiss, every touch was tender but urgent, full of longing and reassuranc

Afterwards, they lay tangled in the sheets. Tremaine's arm draped over her, and Brielle rested her head on his chest. Silence hung heavy. Comfortable, broken only by their shared breaths.

"I wish it could stay like this," she murmured. Her fingers

traced the curve of his shoulder.

"It will," he said. "In time. But you need to go back to my mama's house."

Brielle frowned. "Now? Why?"

He reached over the nightstand and grabbed a stack of cash. He held it out to her. "She called me looking for you. I don't need her to come over here."

She stared at him, disbelief and something warmer mixing in her eyes. "You're giving me money… more money?"

"I'm giving you safety," he said firmly. "And peace of mind."

Brielle held his gaze for a second, then slowly shook her head. "You know I'm not here for your money, right?"

Tremaine's expression didn't change much, but something in his eyes softened. "I know."

"Because the way you keep reaching in your pocket…" she added lightly, though her voice carried a hint of vulnerability. "You making it real easy for somebody to get the wrong idea."

A small smirk tugged at the corner of his mouth. "Anybody who know me know I don't move careless like that."

She studied him, searching his face. "Still. I don't want you thinking I'm one of them girls."

"One of who?" he asked quietly.

"You know," she said, waving her hand vaguely. "The ones who pop up when they see what you got going on."

Tremaine leaned back slightly, voice calm but sure. "If I

thought that's what you was, you wouldn't be sitting here."

That landed.

Brielle's eyes dropped for a second before she slipped the money into her bag, a little slower this time.

They dressed slowly, teasing touches and soft laughs breaking the tension. Tremaine grabbed her hand and lead her down the narrow staircase. He kept one arm around her waist as if he could shield her from the world. Tremaine stood at the door and watched her get into the cab that waited outside.

She turned just before the car pulled away. "I'll see you soon?"

"Hell, yeah," he said.

The cab drove off, city lights reflecting in her eyes. Tremaine leaned against the doorframe, chest tight, knowing that love and the streets never made a clean mix. But he couldn't stay away. And for Brielle, he wouldn't.

Chapter Ten

Tremaine stared at the ceiling like it owed him answers. "Damn," he said, pushing himself up. "You really done took over my whole house."

Brielle laughed from the bathroom. "You'll live."

"Nah," he said, already breaking down his blunt. "My pillows smell like you. My couch smells like you. Soon as you leave, I'm wide awake."

She stepped out of the bathroom in a tank top, hair loose, skin still warm from the shower. No jeans yet. Just standing there like she knew exactly what she was doing.

"Sounds personal," she said.

"And because I sleep better when you here," he added quieter, "house feels off when you not."

She leaned against the doorframe. "You're the one who said I could bounce back and forth."

"Yeah," he admitted. "Didn't know it was gonna hit like this."

She reached up and started tying her hair back.

He frowned. "Why you tying your hair like that? You about to fight somebody?"

She smirked. "Maybe I am."

"Mm hmm," he said. "Look like you gearing up for battle."

"I am," she said, rolling her eyes. "Me and you got business to take care of."

He blinked, confused, because she been on one lately. "So, this what you do now? Come to my house and bully me for dick?"

She laughed. "Don't act like you don't like it."

He shook his head, already smiling. "Yeah," he said. "And now I can't sleep without you."

He held her close in his arms. "You always do that," he said quietly. "Act tough like you don't know how much you got me."

She slid her hands up his chest. Slow. Familiar. "Because every time I say it out loud, you look at me like you scared."

"I'm not scared," he said. "I just don't wanna mess this up."

Her voice softened. "Too late. I already care."

That did it.

He kissed her. Unhurried, like he was memorizing her. Like sleep, peace, and home were wrapped up in one person. They moved together without rushing, laughter mixing with whispers, hands learning what they already knew.

"I like being here," she said against his shoulder. "With you."

He held her tighter. "That's why the house don't feel right when you gone."

She smiled, tracing circles on his back. "You know you stuck with me now."

He laughed under his breath. "Good. Because I don't wanna unstick."

Later, when the room went quiet and the world slowed down, she curled into him like she belonged there.

His phone buzzed like it had no respect for sleep.

"Ma," Tremaine groaned when he picked up and rolled onto his back. "It's early."

"Well, you up," his mother said. "Your sister's party is soon. I need chairs, trays, balloons, and don't forget the cake."

He sighed. "You could've said good morning first."

"Boy, go get dressed," she snapped. "I'll see you soon."

He hung up and looked over at Brielle pulling on her tank top.

"You leaving already?" He asked. "You don't have to."

She smiled but shook her head. "I do."

That answer didn't sit right. He watched her for a second, then stood and walked into the closet.

"What are you doing?" She asked.

He came back holding keys. "Since you heading to my mom's house anyway, and she just called me to pick up stuff for the party, we might as well do that together."

She blinked. "Together?"

"Yeah," he said. "I gotta go there regardless."

She glanced down at the keys in his hand, her brow furrowing. "What keys are those?"

"For you," Tremaine said simply. "Tomorrow you not taking

no bus. There's a black Ford Focus in the garage. It's yours."

Brielle's face changed instantly.

Guard up. Walls back in place.

She looked from the keys…to him…then back again.

"That's…a lot, Tremaine."

He leaned against the counter, unbothered. "It's transportation."

She let out a soft breath that almost sounded like a laugh. "You real casual about life changing gestures."

His mouth twitched slightly. "You real dramatic about accepting help."

Her eyes narrowed just a little. "No. I'm careful."

The room went quiet for a beat.

Brielle crossed her arms loosely, studying him. "Nobody does something like this for me without wanting something."

Tremaine nodded once, like he'd been waiting on that.

"I already told you," he said evenly. "I'm not them dudes. I'm not buying favors. That's lame."

She grabbed her bag. "Come on. Let's go before your mom goes crazy."

As he headed to the bathroom, Tremaine caught his reflection. Brielle moved different. Careful. Intentional. Like she knew where she was going.

The thought hit him out of nowhere.

He could see her as a wife.

He turned on the sink, shaking his head with a quiet laugh.

Not today, though.

Today was about chairs, balloons, and preparing his sister's party.

Chapter Eleven

Brielle was smiling before she even realized it. Tremaine hadn't said it. Hadn't put a title on it. But she felt it anyway. Felt it in how he moved around her. In how he made space. In how he showed up without asking.

She was already his. And somehow, they both knew it.

When he came out the bathroom, towel slung over his shoulder, he caught her staring.

"What?" He asked. "Why you smiling like that?"

She shrugged. "I can't smile now?"

He eyed her. "You smiling at me."

"Maybe," she said. "Problem?"

He smirked, grabbed his wallet and keys off the dresser. "You ready?"

"Been ready," she replied.

Before leaving, he reached under the bed and pulled out his gun, checking it quick before sliding it into his waistband.

Brielle froze. "Is that really necessary?"

"With the life I live?" He said casually. "Hell, yeah."

She followed him out the room. "That's not cute, Tremaine."

"I never said it was," he replied, shutting off the air. "I said it was real. I'm not an average dude. Plenty people would love to see me gone."

"That's even more reason for you to leave the streets alone."

He paused, then nodded once. "You're not wrong."

Outside, he opened the garage. "Bring the Ford out."

"The Ford?" She repeated.

The garage door lifted and Brielle stopped breathing.

Black. Shiny. Brand new. Sitting there like it had been waiting for her.

"No," she whispered. "You did not."

She walked to it slow, hand hovering before touching the door. Slid into the seat like it might vanish if she blinked too hard.

Leather. Screens. Buttons everywhere.

She turned the key. The engine purred.

"Oh, my God," she laughed, half shocked, half overwhelmed.

She eased the car out and Tremaine walked up to the window.

"Thank you!" She squealed, smiling so hard her face hurt.

He shook his head, trying not to let it show, but that smile got him.

"Don't wreck my investment," he said.

She laughed. "You sound like you planning long-term."

"Maybe I am," he replied, low, already knowing that smile was gonna stay with him all day.

Brielle was still discovering things when his phone rang.

She pressed buttons, adjusted the seat, laughed under her breath when the steering wheel moved exactly where she wanted it. "Oh, this is nice" she murmured, running her hand over the dash.

"Told you," Tremaine said distractedly, phone already to his ear.

"Did you find Brielle yet?" His mom asked, no greeting.

"Yeah, ma. We together," he replied. "We about to hit the mall. You need something from her?"

"I just wanted to know where she was at."

"We about to get the stuff you wanted. Anything extra while you're on the phone?" He asked, irritation creeping in.

"Stop by Party City. I need plates, napkins, silverware, tablecloths. Cake we'll get later."

"Alright," he said.

"Don't be late."

He hung up and slid into the passenger seat. "I see you already done figured everything out in here."

She grinned. "It wasn't hard. This car is smart. I like smart things."

"You ready?" He asked.

She glanced at the clock. 11:45 a.m. Her smile softened just a little. "Yeah. I just wanna be back by five. I got schoolwork."

He buckled up and leaned back. "You always thinking ahead."

"Somebody has to."

She pulled off smoothly. For a minute, neither of them spoke. The silence thickened, not awkward, just heavy.

She cleared her throat. "So…"

He glanced over. "So."

She took a breath. "Did you make up your mind about us?"

He watched the road ahead. "Why you want this so bad?"

"Because I love you," she said quietly. "I have for years. And I don't wanna be one of your women. I wanna be your one and only."

Her voice cracked. Tears came before she could stop them.

"Don't cry," he said quickly. "I'm just saying…a woman like you don't need a dude like me."

She laughed through the tears, sharp. So, I'm good enough to fuck but not good enough to be with?"

Her words hit him hard like a ton of bricks.

"Pull over."

Her heart jumped, but she did.

He leaned over and kissed her, slow, and intentional. When he pulled back, he didn't let go of her hand.

"You really want to be my woman?" He said while staring into her soft brown eyes.

"Yes," she said without hesitation, staring back at him.

"You doing something positive with your life," he said, eyes dropping. "I don't wanna mess that up."

She lifted his chin. "Why do you think you would do that? We could build something. Together."

That feeling hit him again. The one he kept shoving down. Being done with the streets. Owning shit. Coming home to one woman. Actually living life and not just existing.

He looked at her. Really looked with deep intention.

"Before, you were a cute, skinny teenage girl," he said honestly. "Now you a beautiful, intelligent, grown woman. I stayed away because of the choices I made with my life. But if you choosing me…"

He squeezed her hand.

"Then I'm choosing you."

She stared at him like he'd lost his mind.

He smiled, leaned in, and kissed her softly. Certain.

"Yes," he said against her lips. "We can be together. I just gotta get some shit straight now."

"Really, baby?" She asked, searching his face.

He nodded.

Her whole face lit up. No hiding it. No trying to be cool.

"You won't regret it," she said, turning the key and pulling back onto the road, heart racing faster than the car.

Chapter Twelve

Brielle parked the Ford and jumped out, her eyes wide. "This place is huge! I could get lost in here for days."

Tremaine followed, stretching. "Don't get lost. Party store first."

She grinned.

He let her go ahead, keeping an eye on the aisles. That's when he saw her. Tawanna, leaning against the candy racks, arms crossed, attitude dialed up to eleven.

"I knew that was you, Stacks!"

Tremaine's jaw tightened. "What's good, Tawanna?" He said calmly, stepping closer. Brielle was near, and he wasn't letting her get caught up in this.

"I've been looking everywhere for you! People thought you got knocked!"

"What you want?" He asked, his tone sharp, scanning for Brielle.

"Ummm…so you getting me pregnant isn't your business?"

Tremaine froze. Then he laughed low, almost cruel. "Really? You still playing that game?"

"I said I'm pregnant!" She yelled, slapping her stomach.

"That ain't my problem. Find your baby's father. It ain't me," he said flat. He saw Brielle, grabbed her hand, and pulled her behind him.

"Wait—so she the reason you denying my baby?" Tawanna pressed.

Tremaine ignored her, tugging Brielle closer. "Move," he said. "We're done here."

Brielle's heart raced, conflicted. should we—"

"No. You trust me, right?" He asked, not looking at her. "Then we go. Now."

Tawanna opened her mouth. "So, you slept with her?"

Tremaine's hand tightened on Brielle's. "Yeah. That's all you need to know. And honestly…" His voice dropped, sharp and cold. "You knew exactly what I'm about. Don't act like it's new. You knew."

Brielle let out a shaky breath, eyes meeting his. She wanted to be mad, but she understood. He wasn't explaining, wasn't apologizing.

He guided her toward the exit, hand firm on her back. "Let's finish this run, get the stuff, and leave."

At the register, Brielle counted cash, still tense but managing a small smile. "I don't get mad easy…but damn, today was a lot."

Tremaine smirked, tugging her hand as they walked out.

Even through the chaos, Brielle understood the life she'd

signed up for with him, the streets, the danger, the unpredictability. And she chose it anyway.

Nothing else mattered. Not the mall. Not the past. Not Tawanna. Just them. And for Brielle, that was enough.

***

Tremaine leaned back in the Ford's driver's seat and let out a long sigh as Brielle put the bags in the car. Women were a headache, and one was easier than many. He just hoped none of his past mistakes would come back to bite him. Tawanna claiming she was pregnant? That was the last straw.

He pulled out his phone and dialed Twin.

"Yo," Twin answered immediately.

"My dude, guess who I just ran into claiming she's pregnant by me?"

"Damn…can't guess. You done been with mad broads."

"You right!" Tremaine laughed, shaking his head. "Remember that chick, Tawanna?"

"Naw…not that one! You hit that, too?"

"Yeah," Tremaine admitted. "And now she's tryna say I knocked her up."

"Damn, my G. That's crazy."

"That ain't my problem. It ain't mine," Tremaine said, chuckling.

Twin laughed too. "Where you at? I gotta hit up Josie's for my wife. She's driving me crazy with cravings."

"I'm about to head there. We could link."

"Bet. See you in a few."

Tremaine hung up and spotted Brielle approaching.

"You good?" He asked, taking the phone from his ear.

"I'm fine," she replied, arms folded, a little frown still lingering.

"I don't like you looking like that. What I gotta do to make you smile?"

He rubbed her thigh gently.

Her eyes softened, glistening. "Tremaine…I want this to work. I don't want you seeing me as a little girl or your sister's friend. I'm a grown-ass woman doing grown woman things."

"I know that. Got it, Ms. Grown-Ass Woman," he said with a smirk.

Taking her hand, he eased the car back onto the road. "Look, I'm not trying to ruin your life. My lifestyle isn't ideal for what you're building, but I'm willing to do this with you. Be stable, settle down…it won't happen overnight, though. You have to be patient."

"I am," she said, squeezing his hand.

"Good. We'll be good."

She tilted her head. "Any other baby mama drama I should know about?"

"I don't have kids. Not my style to abandon one I know is mine," he replied, eyes on the road.

"Okay, so we're good then" she said mockingly, pressing a quick kiss to his cheek. "Where we headed?"

"My mom wants a cheesecake. Josie's."

"I know exactly where that is," she said.

The ride was quiet after that, but the tension had shifted. Brielle still had that little frown, but she understood who Tremaine was. The streets, the past, the danger, but she accepted it.

Minutes later, they pulled up next to Twin's car. Tremaine grabbed Brielle's hand, giving it a reassuring squeeze, and together they headed into Josie's, the world and all its chaos temporarily forgotten.

Chapter Thirteen

Josie's stayed smelling like sugar and nostalgia. The kind of place where everybody had a memory and Tremaine had zero self-control. He leaned over the glass case, already locked in.

"Red velvet," he said like it was a commandment.

Brielle laughed. "You didn't even look at the other cakes."

"I don't cheat," he said. "Not on cake."

"Yo, what's good, my G?"

Tremaine turned and grinned. "What's good?" He and Twin slapped hands, pulling each other in quick. "This my girl, Brielle."

Brielle reached out. Twin shook her hand, sizing her up without being rude about it.

Tremaine leaned close to her. "Can you grab the strawberry cheesecake for my mom and that red velvet for me?"

She nodded and headed to the counter.

Twin watched her walk away, then smirked. "Shorty gotta be serious if you wifed her."

"She is," Tremaine said, pride creeping into his voice before he could stop it

Twin blinked. "Hold up. That little girl that used to be at your mom's crib? Glasses, braces. Ayesha's friend."

"Yeah," Tremaine said, smiling to himself.

"Crazy," Twin said, pulling him into a hug. "I told you there were better women than the ones you was messing with."

Tremaine exhaled. "I just don't know how this ends. She's wanted me since she was a kid."

Twin shrugged. "Then don't overthink it. You ain't never gonna understand women anyway. What's up with Ayesha?"

"She coming home." Tremaine said. I'm tired, bro. I want out. I just want peace."

Twin's jaw tightened. "That ain't on you. Ayesha grown. Still don't know where she even got Molly."

"I wish I did," Tremaine said.

Brielle came back with both cakes. Tremaine took them, careful like they were fragile.

"We'll talk later," Twin said. "Ya'll should come by the crib. My wife's nine months pregnant, on bed rest. She bored."

"That sounds nice," Brielle said. "It was good meeting you."

"Ok, cool" Tremaine said. "I gotta get this to my mama before she flips."

In the car, Brielle leaned back and sighed.

"What's that?" Tremaine asked, reaching for her hand.

"School," she admitted. "I'm behind."

"Then handle that," he said. "I got my mom."

"You sure?"

He kissed her knuckles. "Always."

****

Back home, Keri stood at the mailbox like she'd been waiting.

"About time," she said.

"Go inside," Tremaine told Brielle. "I'll take her."

Brielle smiled, kissed Keri, and disappeared inside.

Keri slid into the passenger seat. "You lying about something."

Tremaine adjusted his seat, already tired. "Where we going?" Ignoring her comment.

"The supermarket."

He started the car, jaw tight. Some days freedom felt close. Other days, it felt like traffic you couldn't beat.

Chapter Fourteen

By the time Tremaine pulled back up to his mother's house, his patience was gone. Completely tapped out. Three hours in the store. Another hour trapped in line. Now the trunk looked like a wholesale warehouse and his phone said it was after six.

He cut the engine and stared straight ahead for a second like that might calm him down. It didn't.

"So, where you putting all this?" He asked, popping the trunk. "And when is this party anyway?"

"Next Friday night," Keri said, already halfway out the car. "Gives me time to cook and lets your sister see everybody."

Her tone was sharp, not aimed at him exactly, but close enough. She disappeared inside and came back dragging a dolly like she was on a mission.

"I'm getting this before my back reminds me how old I am," she muttered.

Tremaine leaned against the car and called Brielle.

"Hello?" She answered, four rings later.

"Dang, took you long enough," he joked.

"Boy, anyway. What's wrong?"

"You finish your work?"

"Most of it. Where you at?"

"Outside. My mom is already irritated. I can hear it in her breathing."

"You want me to come help?"

"Nah. Finish up," he said, stretching his shoulders.

Seconds later, Brielle appeared anyway.

"Like I was really gonna miss time with my man," she said, smiling.

Just like that, his mood shifted.

Keri came back out. "You didn't have to come out here, baby."

"I wanted to," Brielle said, grabbing bags.

"Mama, I got it," Tremaine said. "Go sit down."

"This is too much for you alone," Keri argued.

Brielle slid in smooth. "Why don't you take what you need now and we'll bring the rest?"

Keri sighed. "Fine. I'm cooking. You staying?"

Tremaine looked at Brielle. She nodded.

"Yeah."

"I'm proud of you," Brielle whispered once they were alone.

"For what?"

"You didn't argue."

"We been arguing since the Ayesha incident," he said.

Inside, Keri waved them off. "Go do something till dinner."

Tremaine didn't hesitate to go upstairs. Brielle followed

slowly, knowing exactly what she was doing.

"What are you thinking?" She asked.

He smirked. "Not that."

She laughed. "Liar."

In her room, he got serious. "Homework. Finish it."

"Help me?"

He sat. "What class?"

"American Presidency."

He read the question and frowned. "Who can change the presidency? That's wild."

She answered without blinking. Watching her think did something to him.

Dinner interrupted them.

She walked out smiling. And for the first time in a long time, Tremaine believed in the future.

Chapter Fifteen

When the couple got downstairs, the smell of soul food hit them.

"Damn, it smells good in here," Tremaine said

"Take a seat," Keri instructed.

Once everyone was seated, Keri said, "Ayesha's coming home next week. I'm picking her up after work around four. I'd appreciate it if the two of you could spend some time with her so she doesn't relapse."

Tremaine didn't respond. He was willing to take a couple of days off for his sister.

"I'll definitely make time for her," Brielle said.

Dinner passed in silence until Tremaine's phone rang. He stood up.

"Mama, I gotta go, but thanks for dinner. See you later," he said, running out the door.

Answering the phone, he braced himself.

"Yo, man, meet me at my crib. I got something you need to hear," Darius said.

Tremaine knew Darius wouldn't say more over the phone—

he was paranoid about the Feds listening.

"I'm on my way," Tremaine said, hanging up. He didn't have his car and didn't want to take Brielle's Ford, knowing she needed it for school. He sent a quick text to Brielle.

"Sorry for running out like that. Have something I need to handle. I love you."

He then called Twin.

"Yo."

"Where you at?"

"About to leave the crib, meet Darius."

"Pick me up from my mom's house. I don't have my car."

"Alright, I'll be there in five."

Disconnecting, Tremaine scrolled through a flood of messages—most from unknown numbers. One read, *"Fuck you and your bitch."*

Assuming it was Tawanna, he called the number.

"I see you got my message," she said.

"You just don't get it, do you?" Tremaine replied, annoyed.

"How can you just leave and not say shit?"

"I told you not to catch feelings." He spotted Twin's car and walked up to it.

"You did, but I didn't take you seriously," she said.

"That's on you," he replied.

"Do you think we could…be together one more time? I'll make it worth your while."

Tremaine shook his head. Commitment to Brielle came first. "I'm good. Stop with your calls and texts." He hung up.

"What's good?" He asked Twin.

"Darius said he's got something to tell us. This better be good—my wife went off when I said I was leaving," Twin said, shaking his head.

"Let's see what this crazy motherfucker has," Tremaine said, strapping in. They headed to Darius's.

Cars crowded the driveway. Tremaine's hand rested on his gun. Twin turned off the car. They approached cautiously.

Tremaine knocked. Darius opened the door. "Come in! I've got a big surprise for you!"

Tremaine followed, unsure what to expect. Darius motioned them to the couch. "Sit. I'll be right back."

When Darius returned, Tremaine stood in disbelief.

"What the fuck is he doing here?" He exclaimed.

"Hello, son," James Williams said calmly.

Twin, sensing trouble, whispered, "You thought this was a good idea?"

"I wanted Tremaine to meet his father and talk. With Ayesha in rehab, all bygones need to be bygones," Darius said, disappearing into the kitchen.

"Yes, I need to talk to you," James said, stepping forward.

"I thought you had twenty-five years," Tremaine said.

"I never went to prison," James replied. Tremaine sank onto

the couch, feeling lightheaded.

"Umm…what does this have to do with me?" Twin asked. "I have a pregnant wife at home, and she's mad I'm here."

"It has a lot to do with you. Sit next to your brother," James instructed. Tremaine and Twin exchanged confused glances.

"Your mother and I had fallen out long before you were born," James began. "She was angry over my affair with her best friend. That affair produced you, Jamal."

Twin's jaw dropped. "You mean he's my brother?" He said while pointing at Tremaine.

"Yes," James said.

"You knew about this?" Twin shouted at Tremaine.

"You're older, so hell no," Tremaine said, growing sick of the lies. "So, you cheat on my mom, have a kid, and…what else?"

"What did your mother tell you? And watch your mouth. I'm still your father, and you'll respect me," James said. "I guarantee she told lies about me."

Twin stormed out, his mind reeling. Tremaine stayed, determined to get answers.

"What else did you do?" He asked James, stepping closer. "Never mind what my mama said. I haven't seen you in thirteen years. Where have you been if you weren't in prison?"

"I was watching over your dumb ass out in the streets," James said. "Why do you think you never got into beef or got arrested?"

Tremaine didn't need to think about it—he was careful out

there.

"Your team is about to fall apart. If I were you, I'd give up your throne and walk away."

"What are you talking about?"

"Come to my house, and we'll discuss it in detail," James said, pointing toward the kitchen. Tremaine sensed Darius had something wild planned—something that could land them all in serious trouble.

His phone rang. Brielle. Relief washed over him. He needed her guidance.

"Hey, baby," he said.

"Are you ok?" She demanded.

"Are you by my mother?" He asked, careful.

"Yes, why?"

"Move away from her and listen closely," he instructed, heading upstairs.

"Okay, I'm away. What's going on?"

"My father's at Darius's house and wants me to go to his place to talk."

"Your father?! Didn't you say he was in jail?"

"That's what I thought. Should I go with him or not?"

"No, not by yourself."

"There's nobody else here besides Darius, and I don't want him coming along."

"I'll come then."

"No, you've got school in the morning."

"And you're standing in a house with a man who apparently lied about his whereabouts for thirteen years!" She yelled.

She was right. "Alright. Come pick me up. I'll text you the address.

"So, ready to go?" James asked when Tremaine went back downstairs.

"Yeah, waiting for my girl to pick me up. We'll follow you back," Tremaine said. "Yo, Darius, we're out."

"What, you don't trust me?" James laughed.

"You said it yourself—don't trust no street dude."

"Alright. I hope you can get your issues resolved," Darius said.

"Thanks for getting us here," James added, hugging Darius.

Darius turned to Tremaine. "When's Ayesha's party?"

"Next Friday night," Tremaine replied.

Darius nodded like he was already planning something reckless.

Tremaine grabbed his keys off the counter. "I'll holla at you later."

He didn't wait for a response. Just turned and headed for the door, the noise of the house fading behind him as he stepped out into the night air.

The door clicked shut at his back.

Cool air hit his face, but the tight feeling in his chest didn't ease.

Something about tonight felt…off.

Headlights swept across the driveway.

Tremaine looked up just as Brielle's car rolled in and came to a slow stop.

Right on time.

He pushed off the porch railing and walked toward her, eyes narrowing slightly.

"I got a bad feeling about this," he muttered.

Brielle glanced at him through the open window, brows pulled together. "About what?"

Tremaine exhaled slowly, one hand resting on the top of her car.

"…Don't even know yet."

She studied him for a second, then asked softly, "So what you want to do now?"

"I want to hear him out, but I don't trust him," he admitted.

"It doesn't hurt to listen, baby," she said.

"Ready?" James asked, approaching the car. "Who's this pretty young thing?"

Brielle stiffened. "I'm Brielle, a friend of Ayesha."

James frowned at the mention of Ayesha. Brielle made a mental note to mention it to Tremaine later.

"Yeah, we're ready," Tremaine said, getting in the car. James handed him the address, which Tremaine plugged into the GPS.

"Harlem?" Brielle gasped.

"That's not happening tonight," Tremaine said, frowning. "I can meet him another time."

"Yo, pops, can we do this another time?" He asked, approaching his father's car.

"Scared of Harlem?" James laughed.

"I'm not scared. I've got early stuff in the morning. Afternoon works," Tremaine said, uneasy.

"Go ahead, take your lovely lady home and handle your business. I'd love more grandkids," James said casually.

"What are you talking about now?" Tremaine asked.

"I have seven grandkids, plus the one your brother is having."

"You're telling me I have more siblings?"

"Yes. Three brothers and a sister from me, and a sister from your mom," James replied.

Tremaine's eyes went wide. He needed confirmation.

"Ayesha isn't your daughter?" He asked.

"No. Since you don't want to come to my house, may I come to yours? I want you to know the whole truth."

"How do I know you're telling the truth?" Tremaine spat.

"You won't, unless you hear it," James replied.

"Follow me to my house. Any funny business and you're out," Tremaine said, anger and suspicion thick in his voice.

"Not a problem," James said.

Tremaine climbed into the car, his mind racing. He remembered growing up, he was envied for living in a two-parent household. Furious and hurt, he braced himself for the truth—whatever it may be.

Chapter Sixteen

When she arrived at the house, Brielle pulled into the driveway and turned off the engine. She wanted to hug Tremaine but wasn't sure how he'd react, so she stayed silent.

"I can't believe this shit," Tremaine whispered.

"What did he say?" Brielle asked.

"He said I have two sisters and three brothers. That Ayesha is not his daughter. And that Twin…is his son."

Brielle gasped. "Do you think it's true?"

"I don't know. The only one who can tell me that is my mama. And if it's true… I'm done with her. How the fuck could she lie about my father's whereabouts? I was seventeen when he left. She left me to figure out how to be a man on my own."

Tremaine stormed out of the car and into the house.

James approached Brielle's car. "I didn't mean to upset him, but he needs to know the truth."

"I understand," Brielle said, walking into the house.

Tremaine sat on the couch, head in his hands. Brielle tried to comfort him, but he pushed her away. Seeing he didn't want to be bothered, she excused herself to the kitchen. James sat down.

"You wanted to talk, so talk," Tremaine yelled, banging the table.

"Son, calm down. I know you're upset," James said nervously.

"Don't tell me what to do! You haven't been around for thirteen years!"

"That wasn't my fault! Your mother didn't want me there!" James yelled back.

Brielle, hearing the shouting, couldn't take it. She ran out the kitchen.

"Stop it!" She screamed. "Ya'll are grown men! Can't you have a civilized conversation? Tremaine, you will listen to everything he has to say. Don't interrupt. And James, tell your story from beginning to end. These bits and pieces aren't helping!"

Tremaine took Brielle's hand, sat her down, and kissed her cheek. "I'm sorry.""

James cleared his throat. "No one's ever spoken to me like that, young lady. But I will do as you wish." He stood and walked over.

"I apologize for not being in your life for thirteen years. But your mother is not who you think she is."

Tremaine flinched at the mention of his mother but said nothing.

"When I met your mother, I knew she was going to be my wife. She was seventeen. I was nineteen. We met on an army base in Brooklyn—she was visiting her uncle. I had just finished basic training. After chasing her for four months, she finally gave in. A year later, we were to be married. I had a bachelor party—Jamal's mom, Teresa, was one of the strippers. I was wasted. I woke up next to her, realized we'd slept together. She came to me three months later, pregnant. She didn't want the baby. I told her to have it, and we'd figure it out.

Your mother and I married as planned. I didn't hear from Teresa again until Jamal was born. She said her parents would raise him, and he wasn't to know I was his father. I agreed. A year later, your mother became pregnant with you. I was ecstatic. Life was perfect—until a video of my bachelor party appeared. Your mother threatened divorce. I admitted the affair, but not Jamal's paternity. Things with her were rocky after that, I knew that your mother was messing around with someone from her job, but I didn't fight her about it cause of my infidelity. Then she had Ayesha, but I still loved her.

When you turned seventeen, your mother said it was time for me to leave. She claimed you could handle life without me. I left. Met a woman who loved me as I am, and built a good life in Harlem."

Tremaine shook his head, questions piling up. "Were you hustling when you were with my mom?"

"Yes. That's how she got the house and the repair shop. She asked me to provide, so I did. I wasn't perfect, but I provided."

"Why did she tell me you got knocked because Alfred snitched on you?"

"I don't know. Maybe it was her excuse. Alfred was my brother…someone killed him."

Tremaine froze. "He was my uncle?"

"Yes," James said. His voice heavy with sadness.

Tremaine's world tilted.

"This…this is messed up," he choked out, dragging his hands down his face. His breathing turned ragged. "All this time…"

Brielle moved closer, her arms wrapping around him as his shoulders started to shake.

James leaned forward, confusion and concern written all over his face. "Son… talk to me. What's going on?"

Tremaine let out a broken laugh that held no humor. He finally looked up. Eyes glassy.

"You really wanna know?" His voice cracked. "Because of the lies my mother fed me, I wanted nothing to do with you. No calls. No visits. Nothing."

James went still.

Tremaine swallowed hard. Jaw tight. "She had me thinking you was the worst kind of man. Said you chose the streets over me. Said you ain't care whether I ate or not."

James's face twisted with pain. "That ain't—"

"I know that now," Tremaine cut in, voice rough. "But back then? I hated you, Pops. For years…I hated you."

The word Pops hit the room heavy.

Brielle tightened her hold on him as his voice dropped lower.

"And then she told me why you got locked up." His hands curled into fists. "Said Uncle Alfred snitched to the Feds about your drug activity."

James froze.

The air in the room turned sharp.

Tremaine's voice broke completely. "So, I found him…out in the street…"

His eyes squeezed shut.

"…and I killed him."

Silence crashed down.

Brielle held her breath.

James didn't move. Didn't blink. Just stared at his son like the words hadn't fully landed yet.

"You…what?" James's voice came out hoarse.

Tremaine leaned back in the chair, no guilt on his face this time—just a cold calm that made the room feel smaller.

"Yeah," he said flatly. "I did it."

James staggered back a half step, pain flashing hot across his face.

"You killed my brother," he said quietly, but the hurt underneath it shook the words.

James stepped closer, anger and hurt mixing in his eyes. "You think revenge makes you a man?"

Tremaine met his stare without flinching. "Nah. I just wanted him gone."

Silence stretched between them, thick and ugly.

Finally Tremaine added, colder now, "And honestly… I didn't do it for you."

For a long moment, it looked like James might explode. His fists clenched tight at his sides, chest rising and falling hard.

"That was my right hand," James said, voice thick. "That was my blood. Losing Alfred damn near broke me."

Tremaine whispered, "If I could take it back"Knowing what I know now I wish I could take it back"

James held up a hand, breathing deep like he was wrestling something heavy inside himself.

Finally, his shoulders sagged.

"But you didn't know the truth," James said slowly. His voice was still rough, but the edge had softened. "You was moving off what your mother put in your head."

Tremaine looked up. Eyes full of regret.

"That don't make it right," James continued. "But…I understand why you did what you did."

The words seemed to crack something open in Tremaine.

Before he could stop himself, James stepped forward and pulled him into a tight hug.

Tremaine broke completely then, gripping his father like a little boy who'd been carrying too much for too long.

And for the first time in years…

Neither of them pulled away.

Brielle quietly scooted out of the way and watched the moment unfold. A lump formed in her throat. She wished her own family showed her that kind of grace.

After a moment, Tremaine pulled back. "Can I ask one more question?"

"Ask me anything," James said.

"Why tell me the truth now?" Tremaine asked, looking him dead in the eyes.

James nodded. "I've been living in Harlem since your mother told me to leave. I stopped hustling, but I still hear things. A name kept coming up—Stacks. I didn't connect it to you until I ran into your boy, Darius."

James's jaw tightened. "That man is going to get you killed if he doesn't do it himself."

"What are you talking about?" Tremaine said sharply.

"He's not just hustling," James replied. "He's robbing people. And he's raping women."

"That's bullshit," Tremaine snapped. "I'd know that."

"I got proof." James pulled out his phone. "He raped my neighbor's daughter. She got a picture of him. Am I lying now?"

Tremaine and Brielle looked at the screen.

Brielle's body went stiff.

Her breath caught. She closed her eyes and buried her face into Tremaine's chest, shaking.

"What's wrong?" Tremaine asked, lifting her face.

She couldn't speak.

James continued, unaware. "He's wanted in New York City. I used him to get to you, and it was easy. Too easy. He walked me right into your house. I could've been anyone."

Tremaine barely heard him now. His focus was on Brielle's tears.

"Talk to me," he said softly.

Brielle opened her mouth, trembling.

What she was about to say was about to tear Tremaine's world wide open.

Chapter Seventeen

"Is that…Darius?" Brielle whispered, her voice shaking.

"Yeah," Tremaine said, his jaw tight.

Brielle's hands trembled. "He…he raped and robbed me a couple months ago. He said if I ever told, he'd kill me."

James shot up with his fists clenched. "That bastard has to be stopped. You can't trust him with anything."

Tremaine pulled Brielle into his arms, "I'm sorry…I'm so sorry," he repeated over and over. Her body shook against his chest. The news ignited a fire in him. He knew then he had to get out of the streets—alive. Every lie, every betrayal from people he trusted flashed through his mind.

"How can I leave the game and not die doing it?" He asked, voice low.

James's expression hardened. "Once you're in, you're in. Dealing drugs isn't a joke. The higher up you are, the harder it is to walk away. You run the team—direct the sales, manage the connects, make sure the product's right. You've never done the dirty work yourself, but that doesn't make it easy to leave."

Tremaine's eyes narrowed. "You did it. Why can't I?"

"Are you ready to trade this life for a real one? Work all day—no fast cars, no jewelry, no easy money? Once you leave, there's no turning back. You'll have to relocate."

"I'm ready," Tremaine said. "Now tell me how."

James nodded. "You can buy your way out to whoever's at the top. Or, if you're straight with them, have a talk. They might let you walk."

Tremaine rubbed his face. "Alright…I'll think about it. I'm calling it a night. I'll holla at you later."

"Okay," James said, giving Brielle a reassuring nod. "Don't worry. Darius's going to get his."

They walked James to his car. Brielle was still pale, haunted by the photo she had seen. Tremaine held her close.

"It's okay, baby. I won't let anyone hurt you," he whispered when they were back inside.

"How can you be so sure? You won't always be around," she said, tears streaming.

"You're right. I won't." He pulled out his gun, laid it on the table, and emptied the chamber. "I'll take you to the range. I'll teach you to use one."

Brielle stared at the gun. "I've never even held one."

"And we'll pray you never have to." Tremaine took her hand and led her upstairs. "Get some sleep. You've got school tomorrow."

He stripped off his clothes, lit a blunt, and exhaled slowly.

Brielle climbed onto the bed, still haunted by the memory of Darius's attack—and the image of her brother, her first abuser. Her heart ached. All men, she thought bitterly, just lie. She stripped down to her bra and underwear and curled up into a ball.

Tremaine finished his blunt, turned off the light, and lay beside her, holding her as she cried softly. He wanted to kill Darius for what he did but thought better of it. No plan. No backup. Not yet.

** *****

Tremaine's mind drifted back eighteen years ago. He was twelve, standing on a corner, watching Darius make his first crack sale. Latest Jordans on, gold glinting in the sun. Tremaine wanted in. He approached, calm.

"What's good, man?" He asked.

Darius sized him up. "Who sent you to my block?"

"Nobody sent me."

"What the fuck you want, then?" Darius spat but lowered the gun.

"I want to roll with you."

"Get the fuck out, homie. Once you're in, you're in forever," Darius warned.

"No shit," Tremaine spat back. "You gonna let me rock, or not?"

****
****

Tremaine opened his eyes. "What the fuck?" He whispered. Brielle was asleep beside him. Sweat clung to his back. He shook her lightly.

"Mmm," she moaned. "What time is it?"

"It's six."

"Damn…I gotta get up now." She groaned and moved toward the bathroom. "My first class starts at eight forty."

"Wanna join me?" She asked with a sly smile.

"Right behind you, baby," Tremaine said, following her.

Chapter Eighteen

Brielle stepped into the shower, letting the warm water wash over her. Tremaine followed, wrapped his arms around her, and held her close as she rested her head on his chest. He grabbed a rag, soaped it up, and began washing her.

Tremaine felt himself falling deeper in love. Every second with her reminded him why he had to walk away from the streets—even if it meant starting over with nothing.

"We gotta leave once I leave the game," he said.

"I know…I don't know where to go" she sighed. Memories of upheaval weighed on her.

"We'll figure it out. Trust me?" He asked and kissed her lips.

"Okay…I trust you," she said. She turned around and pressed herself against him.

The intimacy escalated quickly, a mix of desperation and love. Their shared connection drowned out all the chaos outside. When it was over, Brielle stepped away to rinse off and catch her breath.

"I have to go," she said as she stepped out of the shower.

Tremaine rinsed himself, grabbed a towel, and followed her. "I'll take you to school," he said as he checked the clock: seven-thirty.

Brielle hurried to get dressed. "You better not have gotten me pregnant with that stunt," she warned.

"What stunt?" He asked with a grin.

"I'm serious! I have school to finish."

"You'll finish school. And even if…it doesn't matter. I'm not going anywhere."

"Let's not talk about a baby, please."

"You got everything?" He asked.

"Phone, keys, wallet…books are in the car," she said, following him.

"Want to eat before you go?"

"No time. I'll pick something up," she replied, opening the door. Tremaine made sure he had his essentials and locked up.

"You alright?" He asked.

"Yeah…just get me to school." She smirked.

The drive was quick. Brielle gathered her things to leave.

"Damn, not even gonna say bye?" He teased.

"Bye," she said, smiling and pressing a tender kiss to his lips.

He watched her walk inside, then called Twin.

"What the fuck was that last night?" Twin demanded.

"The truth of our lives," Tremaine said, starting the car.

"Where you at?" Twin asked.

"About to hit the gym."

"I'll meet you there," Twin said.

Tremaine's phone rang. It was his mother. He spat under his breath. "Fuck that bitch." The revelation about Darius and his father's story had shattered his trust.

At the gym, Twin's car was parked out front. Tremaine made sure his gun was ready and stepped inside.

"What's goodie?" Twin greeted.

"You look like hell," Tremaine said.

Twin rubbed his face. "I ain't sleep. Last night got my head messed up."

Tremaine studied him. "Yeah…same here."

Twin let out a short breath. "Man, this still don't sound real. We really related?"

"I don't know what's real or fake anymore?" Tremaine shot back.

"I don't know what to think," Twin muttered.

Tremaine crossed his arms. "You remember people always saying we looked alike?"

Twin paused. "…Yeah."

"Wasn't just talk," Tremaine said.

Silence stretched.

"You good with this?" Twin asked.

Tremaine gave a small shrug. "I been dealing with worse this week."

That pulled the faintest smirk from the twin.

"…Aight then," he said quietly. "Guess we figuring this out."

Tremaine nodded once.

"Yeah," he said. "Guess we are."

"Tell me…you heard anything about Darius," Twin asked. Lowering his voice, Tremaine said, "Dad said he's robbing and raping women. Brielle confirmed it."

"What?! Her?" Twin asked, eyes wide.

"Yeah. I want to kill him for hurting her."

"You can't," Twin warned.

"I know. That's why I'm leaving the game. Packing up and leaving," Tremaine said.

"If you leave, I'm out too. But my family and I can't leave. Not until the baby is born. What about your mom and sister?"

"My mom? She lied about everything," Tremaine said, punching the wall.

"So, your dad wasn't lying last night?" Twin asked.

"You ready to hear the rest of what he said?" Tremaine asked.

"Yeah…I need to know the truth," Twin said, abandoning his workout. "Let's go."

"So, what happened after I left?" Twin asked.

Tremaine explained. "He told me about my mom, the bachelor party, how they met, my mom finding out about the affair…all of it. Dad left because my mom forced him out."

Twin shook his head. "Ayesha isn't your dad's?"

"Nope. Crazy, right?" Tremaine sighed. "I'm telling Ayesha the truth today."

"You think that's a good idea?"

"She's twenty. She deserves to know who her father is and that her mom's a liar."

"Maybe after the party," Twin suggested.

"Yeah…that makes sense," Tremaine agreed, gripping the steering wheel.

He drove toward the hospital, nerves twisted in his stomach. The world felt like it was collapsing, and he couldn't wait to leave Newark and start fresh.

Chapter Nineteen

The visit with Ayesha went better than Tremaine expected. She looked healthier than the night he brought her in. Her color was returning and her eyes were clearer. Even though she wasn't excited about rehab, she agreed to go just to please their mother. Still, Ayesha noticed something was off with Tremaine. He wasn't himself. She made a mental note to press him when they got home.

Checking his watch, Tremaine sighed. "I gotta hit the road, sis."

"Tremaine, what's wrong with you?" Ayesha asked. His face gave him away.

Tremaine looked to Twin for backup. Knowing Tremaine couldn't lie to save his life, Twin stepped in. "Your brother's just worried about you. He wants you better," he said, pulling Ayesha into a hug.

Tremaine exhaled in relief. But Ayesha was just like their mother—she'd nag until the truth spilled.

"No. That's not it," Ayesha snapped, staring straight at Tremaine. "Why you keeping secrets from me?"

"Ayesha, you can't handle the truth," Tremaine said quietly.

"You're right!" She screamed. "That's why I'm in here. Reality is a bitch. Everybody lies to me like I'm stupid!"

She broke down and appeared to be spiraling fast.

Twin grabbed her gently and laid her back on the bed. "What happened, Ayesha? What pushed you here?"

"My mother is a liar," she sobbed. "The man I thought was my father isn't my father."

Tremaine froze.

"A man came to the house months ago," she continued. "I asked who he was and he said he was my father. I demanded my birth certificate from mom. She slapped me and said I was crazy. But I look just like him. I know she lied."

She shot up. "Who is he, Tremaine?"

"I don't know who he is," Tremaine admitted. "But if he said he's your father…he might be telling the truth."

"So, you knew and didn't tell me?" She screamed. "I hate you!"

"Calm down," Twin said firmly.

"This has nothing to do with you!" She yelled and shoved him. "You're not family!"

"He's our brother," Tremaine snapped. "So, it has everything to do with him. You need to be mad at mom. She lied to all of us."

Ayesha collapsed again. "I don't wanna go home with her."

"Where you gonna go?" Tremaine asked.

"I don't know…"

Twin sighed. "We got bigger problems. Family lies—and Darius."

Ayesha looked up. "What about Darius?"

"He raped Brielle," Tremaine said flatly.

Ayesha burst into tears. "Please don't tell me it was the night I took her to his house."

Tremaine lunged forward and grabbed her collar. "Why the fuck did you take her there?"

Twin shoved Tremaine back. "Chill. Let her talk."

"He gave me pills," Ayesha cried. "Said they'd make me feel better. I was depressed. I left Brielle alone with him. I didn't know."

"What pills?" Twin asked.

"I don't know."

Tremaine lost it. "You could've died!"

"I thought he was your friend," she whispered.

"No," Tremaine growled. "He hurt people that I love."

Ayesha looked confused. "What do you mean people you love?"

Tremaine sighed. "Brielle and I are together."

Ayesha smiled through tears. "Finally. I'm happy for you."

Twin rubbed the back of his neck and looked at Tremaine sideways. "So…what you thinking?"

Tremaine didn't hesitate. "Darius gotta go."

Twin's head snapped back. "See, this what I mean. You wake

up and choose violence every time."

"I'm serious."

"I can tell," Twin muttered. "That's the problem." His voice hardened. "We not doing nothing till after the party. We move smart, not emotional. Until then, nobody says or does nothing. You hear me?"

Tremaine's jaw tightened, but he gave a short nod.

Ayesha shifted in the bed, already looking annoyed. "So, what about me? I gotta go back to my mom's?"

"For now," Tremaine said.

Her face twisted instantly. "I don't wanna go back over there."

"You'll be alright."

Ayesha's eyes flashed. "Don't do that. Don't brush me off like that."

"I'm not brushing you off. I'm trying to keep you safe."

"Safe?" She let out a sharp breath. "You don't live with her, Tremaine. You don't gotta deal with the attitude, the slick comments, the way she be looking at me like I'm a problem."

Twin glanced between them. "Ayesha…"

"No, because every time something pop off, I'm the one that gotta be uncomfortable," she pressed, voice rising. "It's always 'Ayesha go here, Ayesha stay there.' I'm tired of it."

Tremaine's tone dropped low. "It's temporary."

"You said that last time," she shot back quick. "And the time before that. Temporary be lasting real long when it's me."

Silence fell heavy between them.

Then Ayesha looked at him, eyes sharp. "You taking Brielle with you?"

Tremaine nodded once.

Ayesha let out a dry, hurt laugh and looked away. "Yeah…figured."

"That ain't even like that," Tremaine said, irritation creeping in.

"It look exactly like that," she fired back. "When it's Brielle, you got a whole exit plan. When it's me, it's 'go back to mom's and be patient.'"

Twin stepped forward a little. "Aight, both of y'all—"

"I'm just saying," Ayesha muttered, folding her arms tight. "Don't act like I don't see the difference."

Tremaine stared at her. Frustration written all over his face. "You doing too much right now."

"And you not doing enough," she shot back quick.

Before he could respond, a knock interrupted him.

The nurse stepped in. "Vitals check."

The tension didn't leave. It just paused.

Twin exhaled and backed toward the door. "Yeah…I'mma head home before y'all drag me into this." He pointed at Ayesha. "Love you, lil sis."

She gave a small shrug. "Love you, too."

Tremaine lingered by the door a second longer, eyes still

locked on hers.

Ayesha looked right back, stubborn and unmoved.

"Love you," Tremaine echoed as he followed Twin out the door.

As the door closed, Tremaine felt the weight crushing him. Lies everywhere. Betrayal everywhere.

But one thing was clear.

Darius and his mother were going to be dealt with.

One way or another.

Chapter Twenty

After dropping Twin off, Tremaine glanced at the clock—two in the afternoon. He had a few hours before picking up Brielle, so he went to see someone he hadn't planned on seeing but knew he had to.

Snake.

Snake had been more than a boss. He was a mentor. A street father. The one who shaped Tremaine into the calculated, no-nonsense hustler he'd become.

Tremaine wiped his sweaty palms on his jeans when he pulled into the driveway. What he was about to ask could get him killed. But he wasn't asking for himself anymore. He was asking for Brielle.

She deserved better.

A woman opened the door. "He's waiting for you."

Tremaine walked down the long hallway and entered the last room on the right.

"Have a seat, son," Snake said.

Tremaine sat.

"Cigar?" Snake offered. "Fresh from Cuba."

Tremaine shook his head.

Snake leaned back and puffed smoke into the air. Big. Calm. Dangerous. Cuban accent thick, voice smooth.

"What brings you here today?"

"I need a man-to-man conversation," Tremaine said, locking eyes with him just like Snake taught him.

"Speak."

"I want out of the game."

The words lifted something heavy off his chest.

Snake studied him. "The money not good enough?"

"It's not about money."

"Then what is it?" Snake asked. "I watched you grow up. Your hunger. Your discipline. That's why I put you in charge. Don't tell me you fell in love." Snake laughed.

"I did," Tremaine said calmly. "And I don't feel right living like this anymore."

Snake smiled. "Congratulations. You just became a real man. Real men know when it's time to change. She's lucky."

Tremaine swallowed. "So, what do I have to do?"

"Nothing," Snake said. "You're free. You paid your dues. Eighteen years is a long time."

It felt too easy.

"So, you not sending anyone after me?" Tremaine asked.

Snake laughed so hard he nearly choked. "No. But I do suggest you leave the state. Whatever happens won't come from my camp."

"Thank you," Tremaine said as he stood.

"Anyone else want out?"

Tremaine called Twin and put him on speaker. "Yo. Snake wants to know if you in or out."

"What's good, Snake," Twin said.

"I'm well."

"I'm about to be a father," Twin said. "I want out."

"You two are smart men," Snake replied. "Granted."

Tremaine ended the call and shook Snake's hand.

"Be good to that woman," Snake said.

"I will."

As Tremaine walked out, Snake watched him go. He'd seen all of them grow up. But Tremaine was different. Snake said a silent prayer and returned to his cigar and pool table.

Tremaine left feeling free.

For the first time in his life.

He celebrated the only way he knew how. Jewelry store. Rolex for himself. And for Brielle—a promise ring. A quarter-carat princess cut, white gold. Simple. Elegant. Real.

He smiled to himself. Love really was something else.

When he pulled up to Brielle's school, she was already outside, backpack hanging off one shoulder. Exhaustion written all over her face.

"I thought class ended at five," he said as she slid into the passenger seat.

"Got out early," she sighed. "I needed a break before my brain shut down completely."

He smirked as he pulled off. "When's your last day?"

"Wednesday," she said. "Why?"

He glanced at her. "How you feel about taking a trip?"

Her head snapped toward him. "Where?"

"You got a passport?"

"No."

"Then Puerto Rico it is."

She squealed and grabbed his arm. "You serious?"

"As a heart attack."

They pulled into his mom's driveway a little while later. He parked her car and cut the engine.

"I got you something," Tremaine said, reaching into the console.

Brielle's eyes narrowed. "Why you smiling like that? I don't trust that face."

A small smirk pulled at his mouth. "You always this suspicious?"

"Only when you moving funny," she shot back, but she was already curious.

He placed the small box in her hand. "Open it."

Brielle gave him one more look, then slowly lifted the lid.

She went still.

"…Tremaine."

"It ain't what you thinking," he said quietly, though his voice had softened.

Her eyes lifted to his. "You sure about that?"

Instead of answering, he gently took the ring from the box.

She let out a quiet breath she didn't realize she was holding.

Tremaine reached for her right hand, his touch careful and sure, and slid the ring onto her finger.

"It ain't no pressure," he said low. "Just something real."

Brielle stared down at her hand like she was trying to process it.

Then his voice came again, steady and soft.

"I love you," he said. "And I promise I won't hurt you."

That broke her.

Her hand flew to her mouth before she leaned over and wrapped her arms around him tight.

"You really trying to have me out here emotional," she murmured against him.

Tremaine held her close, a quiet satisfaction in his voice.

"…You happy though?"

Brielle pulled back just enough to look at him, her smile soft but full.

"Yeah," she whispered. "You make me real happy."

"For the rest of the week, I won't really be around," he said. "Until Ayesha comes home."

"That's forever," she pouted.

"I'm handling things. Then it's us."

He kissed her once more. They got out the car

"Get inside before I change my mind and kidnap you."

She laughed, grabbed her bag, kissed him again, and went inside.

Tremaine waited until the door closed before he stepped out. walking down the block.

A cab pulled up a minute later.

As he slid into the back seat, he glanced once more at the house.

For the first time, the future didn't feel heavy.

It felt possible.

Chapter Twenty-One

A time moved so slow that it felt like forever for Brielle and Tremaine. They missed each other like crazy. Tremaine was up with the sun, heading to his mom's house with a mission—and a plan.

Brielle swung the door open, and the second her eyes landed on him, her whole face lit up.

"Well, look who finally decided to show up," she teased, stepping back to let him in.

Tremaine stepped inside and kicked the door shut behind him, sliding the lock with a quick click.

"You lucky I ain't kick the door in," he muttered.

Brielle laughed, bumping his shoulder. "You always gotta be extra."

Ayesha, who had been leaning against the wall scrolling on her phone, looked up slowly. "Why you come in here looking like the police behind you?"

Tremaine didn't answer. He just jerked his head toward the stairs.

"Both of y'all. Come on."

Ayesha's face scrunched up instantly. "Excuse me? I know you not commanding me."

Brielle glanced between them. "Tremaine…what's going on?"

"Upstairs," he said, already starting toward the steps. "Now."

Ayesha sucked her teeth but pushed off the wall. "If this is some nonsense, I'm going right back downstairs."

"Just come on," Tremaine shot back, not even looking at her.

Brielle followed first, curiosity written all over her face. Ayesha came behind them, arms folded tight, attitude fully activated.

By the time they reached his room upstairs, Tremaine pushed the door open and waved them inside.

The second they stepped in, his whole energy shifted.

Serious. Heavy.

Brielle's smile faded. "Okay…you doing too much. What's wrong?"

Ayesha narrowed her eyes at him. "Yeah, because you got that look. I don't like that look."

Tremaine shut the door behind them and finally faced both of them, jaw tight.

"Y'all know some real stuff about to go down, right?"

The room went still.

Ayesha straightened a little, irritation mixing with concern. "Tremaine…what did you do now?"

Brielle's voice came softer. "You scaring me a little."

Brielle crossed her arms, brow pulled tight. "What the hell is going on this time?"

Tremaine lifted both hands like he was trying to keep the peace, but his voice stayed firm. "Simple version. We all gotta act like we don't know nothing about my mom and Darius. No slip ups. No funny looks. Nothing."

Ayesha let out a loud, dramatic groan and tossed her head back. "Oh, my God. So now we actors too? For how long...forever?"

Tremaine shot her a look. "Ayesha, I'm serious."

"I can see that," she muttered, rolling her eyes. "You got your whole serious face on and everything."

But the attitude didn't quite hide the tension sitting on her shoulders.

Across the room, Brielle's grip tightened on her bag, fingers trembling just a little. "I swear...I just want things to stay good." Her voice softened. "I'm finally happy, Tremaine."

That took the edge off his face quick.

He stepped closer and gently cupped her face. "I love you," he said low. "But I got some moves to make. For us."

Brielle leaned into his hands, but her eyes still carried worry.

Behind them, Ayesha made a small noise under her breath.

Tremaine's gaze flicked to her.

She immediately straightened and folded her arms tighter. "What? Don't look at me like that. I'm just standing here."

"You always just standing here with something to say," he muttered.

Ayesha sucked her teeth. "Boy, please. If I start talking for real, your feelings gonna be hurt."

Brielle shot her a look. "Ayesha, not right now."

"I'm just saying," Ayesha replied, but her voice had lost some of its bite. She shifted her weight, clearly uneasy even though she was trying to play it off. "This whole thing feel messy."

Tremaine studied her for a second longer, then nodded once.

"Just…look out for each other while I'm gone," he said. "I'll be back Friday for the party."

Ayesha lifted a brow. "You better be. Because if I gotta keep pretending for days, you owe me food and money."

Despite everything, the corner of Tremaine's mouth twitched.

Brielle, though, still looked worried. And everybody in the room felt it.

Before they could protest, he was gone, slipping out the door like a shadow.

The girls looked at each other and hugged tight. The kind of hug that said everything words couldn't.

Ayesha pulled back just enough to whisper, "Don't worry, Brielle. My brother's got this. Trust me."

Brielle nodded, squeezing Ayesha's hand. "I hope you're right."

****
*****

Friday finally came. Ayesha's party day.

Brielle was buzzing with excitement.

Tremaine was not.

He moved fast, sharp, running errands like he was trying to outrun his own thoughts. Truth was, he was. Anything to avoid being in the same room with his mother longer than necessary.

First stop was Josie's for the vanilla cake with buttercream filling Ayesha swore she needed like oxygen.

By the time they pulled up to meet Twin with Ayesha's cake in front of Josie's, Tremaine's jaw had already been tight for hours.

Twin slid the cake carefully into the backseat, then jerked his chin toward his black Mercedes. "Just follow me. I'm about to drop this and head back to pick up my wife."

"Bet," Tremaine muttered.

They pulled off behind him.

A few seconds passed before Tremaine checked his watch and exhaled hard. "Ayesha about to blow my phone up."

Right on cue, Brielle's phone rang.

She glanced at the screen and smirked. "Speak of the drama queen."

Tremaine didn't even crack a smile.

Brielle tossed him the phone. "It's Ayesha. Answer it before she calls twelve more times."

He caught it and brought it to his ear. "We on our way," he said flatly.

Click.

He hung up before she could start.

Brielle turned slowly in her seat. "Why are you always so mean to her?"

Tremaine kept his eyes on the road. "Because she get on my nerves."

Brielle let out a soft laugh. "You say that every time."

"And I mean it every time."

But the edge in his voice wasn't really about Ayesha.

Brielle peeped it but didn't push. Instead, she shook her head and smiled to herself. Best friends since first grade, she already knew Ayesha was a lot on a good day.

They finally pulled up behind Twin's Mercedes.

Brielle cut the engine and leaned back. "How long this about to take?"

Tremaine watched Twin disappear into the house, his expression going hard again, thoughts clearly somewhere else.

"Not long," he said low. "Soon as he come back out, we gone."

But the way his fingers kept tapping against his thigh said his mind was nowhere near this party.

It was still stuck on his mother.

And Darius.

A few minutes later, a tap on the window made Brielle jump. Tremaine rolled it down.

"We're ready," Twin said.

"Alright, follow us," Tremaine replied, trying to keep his cool—but Brielle immediately sensed the edge in his voice.

"Really? You're doing that thing again," she shot. "The silent treatment mixed with attitude? Seriously, Tremaine, what's your problem?"

He glanced at her. Jaw tight. "Problem? I don't have a problem. I'm just done with drama. That's all I've been dealing with lately."

"Oh, so now you're the martyr?" She fired back. "Everything's drama when it's convenient for you, huh? You can't even tell me what's going on without snapping!"

"I'm not snapping! I'm tired, okay? I've been handling my life, my mess, and somehow, I'm the bad guy?"

"Bad guy?!" Brielle raised her voice and leaned forward. "You think ignoring me and giving me one-word answers counts as handling your life? Newsflash, it's called shutting people out!"

Tremaine slammed a hand on the wheel and exhaled hard. "Damn, Bri! I'm trying to keep my head above water. You think I like feeling like this all the time?"

"Try telling me!" She yelled. "Try telling me instead of acting like I'm the problem every damn time!"

He took a deep breath, gripping the wheel tighter. "Alright, alright! I hear you. I'm…I'm not trying to hurt you. I just—shit, I can't explain it without it turning into an argument every time!"

Brielle crossed her arms but softened slightly, tears brimming.

"All I want is to talk without it blowing up in our faces. Is that too much?"

Tremaine cracked a half-smile and shook his head. "Nope. Not too much. I'll try…for today."

By the time they pulled into the driveway, Brielle had wiped her tears but still wore a stubborn pout. Tremaine jumped out, grabbed the bags, and headed inside. She lingered with Ayesha's cake, waiting for Twin and his pregnant wife to go in before stepping out herself.

Ayesha sidled up. "He's a jerk," she whispered.

Brielle blinked, putting on a casual smile. "What? Nah, we just had a…lively discussion."

Ayesha smirked. "Uh-huh. Sure, lively. Don't pay him mind. Let's have a good time," Ayesha said, holding the door open.

Brielle gave a small smile, then walked over to where Tremaine stood against a wall. Her chest still felt tight from the fight.

Tremaine stepped closer. His hand brushed hers. "Bri…I hate how we fought. I hate it."

She let out a shaky laugh. "Me too. I…I don't want to fight with you ever again."

He cupped her face in his hands and brushed her cheek with his thumb. "You're my world. I don't care how stubborn we get, nothing's ever going to change that."

Her lips trembled as tears formed in her eyes. "I love you, Tremaine. I just…sometimes I'm scared of losing you."

"You're not losing me," he whispered, pulling her into his chest. "I'm not going anywhere. Not now. Not ever."

She buried her face against him, letting the tension and frustration of the fight slip away. "Promise me we'll always talk before it gets this far," she murmured.

"I promise," he said, tilting her chin up to kiss her softly. Their lips lingered, warm and reassuring. "Truce?" He asked when they pulled back.

"Truce," she whispered, hugging him tighter.

Suddenly, the hallway light revealed Keri standing there, eyes wide, mouth slightly open. "Wait…what?"

Brielle jumped back, blushing. "We…we were just—"

Tremaine held her hand protectively. "We just…weren't ready to tell anyone yet."

Keri shook her head, still stunned. "You two…together? And all this time, you were sneaking around?"

Brielle stammered, "we wanted to wait until we knew it was serious."

Tremaine smiled, squeezing Brielle's hand. "It is serious. I love her. I won't let her go."

Keri blinked, her shock slowly softening into a mix of disbelief and curiosity. "Well…I guess that explains a lot."

Brielle laughed nervously.

Keri crossed her arms, shaking her head but smiling reluctantly. You better be serious about her, boy."

"I am," Tremaine said firmly, still holding Brielle close.

"Party started," Keri finally said, trying to regain her composure. "Come on, let's go downstairs…and you two can explain yourselves later."

Brielle followed Tremaine downstairs and froze.

Why was she here? She thought.

Chapter Twenty-Two

Tracey was Brielle's archenemy. A real bitch. She thrived on making Brielle's life miserable.

"What's the matter?" Tremaine asked.

"I forgot my bathing suit. I'll be right back," Brielle said.

"I was looking for you," Ayesha said, noticing Brielle's frown.

"What is that bitch, Tracey, doing here?" Brielle muttered.

"I don't know," Ayesha explained. She noticed Brielle's unease and grabbed her arms. "What's wrong?"

"I'm going to get my bathing suit," Brielle replied, heading upstairs with Ayesha on her heels.

"What's going on between you and Tracey?" Ayesha asked. She'd noticed Brielle's behavior whenever Tracey was around.

"Y'all got beef?" Ayesha pressed.

Brielle sighed. She hadn't wanted to bring this up,

"Tracey is my sister."

The words dropped heavy.

Ayesha blinked once…then twice. "Your what?" She snapped, voice jumping an octave.

"You heard me," Brielle shot back, already reaching for her

swimsuit like she hadn't just flipped the whole room upside down.

Ayesha stared at her. "Since when you got siblings? Because last time I checked, you was out here acting like an only child."

Brielle's shoulders stiffened. "There's a lot you don't know about me," she muttered, tugging her one piece into place.

The room went quiet.

Too quiet.

When Brielle turned back around, she froze.

Ayesha was crying.

Not the cute little watery eyes either. Real tears. Silent and hurt.

Brielle's attitude dropped instantly. "Ayesha...yo, why are you crying?" She rushed over and pulled her into a hug.

Ayesha didn't hug her back at first.

"I can't believe you kept this from me," she choked out. "All these years, Brielle? What else you not telling me?" Her voice cracked. "I thought we was best friends."

Guilt punched Brielle straight in the chest.

"I'm sorry," she said quickly, softer now. "I didn't tell you because…it's not nothing good to tell."

Ayesha pulled back just enough to look at her, eyes red and searching. "Then talk to me."

Brielle swallowed hard, the walls she kept up for years starting to crack.

"Tracey hates me," she said quietly. "My mom was on drugs

heavy. Like…bad. My dad can't stand to look at me because I remind him of her."

Ayesha's face shifted from anger to shock.

Brielle kept going, voice tight but steady. "And my brother…he in jail now. For trying to force himself on me."

Ayesha sucked in a sharp breath. "Brielle…"

"I don't have family like that," Brielle finished, finally meeting her eyes. "Not the kind you brag about. Not the kind you bring around your friends."

Her voice softened even more.

"That's why I was always at your house growing up. It wasn't just because we was besties." She gave a small, sad shrug. "It was because nobody at mine was checking for me."

Silence filled the space.

Heavy.

Honest.

And for the first time, Ayesha saw the parts of Brielle her best friend had been working overtime to hide.

"I'm so sorry. I didn't know," Ayesha whispered, hugging her tightly.

"Don't worry. I've forgiven and moved on," Brielle reassured her. "And now, you're my family. Your brother, you, your mom."

Ayesha headed for the door, then paused. "What about Tracey? Should I kick her out?"

"No. Let her stay. I won't let her upset me today," Brielle said confidently.

By the time Brielle stepped back onto the patio by the pool, her mood was already off.

The air felt…wrong.

Then she saw why.

Tremaine was standing stiff near the railing, and right in front of him was….

Tracey.

Brielle stopped walking.

Tracey's head snapped up, eyes widening. "What are you doing here?"

Brielle let out a slow breath and rolled her eyes hard. "Funny. I was just about to ask you the same thing."

Tremaine looked between them, tension creeping into his shoulders. "Hold up… y'all know each other?"

Tracey's gaze locked onto Brielle, cold and unblinking. "That's my little sister"

The words hit the space like a slap.

Brielle gave a dry laugh. "Oh, now I'm your sister? That's new."

Tracey's mouth tightened. "I didn't come here for you. I came for my homie." She flicked an irritated glance around. "If I knew you was gonna be here, I wouldn't have even pulled up."

"Good," Brielle shot back. "You can still leave."

Tremaine stepped slightly between them, palms half raised.

"Aight…both of y'all need to—"

"Stay out of this," both women snapped at the same time.

The tension spiked.

Tracey took one slow step forward. "You always got something slick to say, don't you?"

Brielle folded her arms, chin lifting. "Only when you around."

For a split second, it looked like Tracey might walk away.

Then her lip curled.

"What you gonna do, Brielle?" She sneered. "Run your mouth like always?"

Before Tremaine could react, Tracey shoved him hard out of the way and launched forward.

And just like that…

All hell broke loose.

Brielle braced herself. The fight was on. Tracey went for her head and punched her repeatedly. Brielle landed blows of her own. When Tracey slipped after a punch to her face, Brielle pounced and refused to back down.

Tremaine tried to separate them. Brielle finally released Tracey and then stood up slowly. He knew he had seconds to get Brielle away.

Tracey, infamous for carrying a razor, lunged. She grabbed Brielle's hair, spitting the blade from her mouth. Tremaine grabbed her wrist, forcing her to drop it. By now, a crowd had gathered.

"T, chill. She's my woman, and I won't let you do this to her. Not now, not ever," Tremaine said, pulling her close.

"Get the fuck out of here with that shit," Tracey laughed.

Brielle had had enough. She slapped Tracey hard. When Tracey fell back, Brielle pounced again. She snatched the razor and she shouted, "I didn't do anything to you, but if you want to cut me, let's go!" They tangled, kicked, and punched until they fell into the pool. Water churned red, and Tremaine knew someone was hurt.

He jumped in and grabbed Brielle. Tracey clutched her wrist and screamed, "this bitch cut me!"

Tremaine managed to pull Brielle free. Ayesha ran up.

"Take her inside!" Tremaine ordered. Brielle protested, but Ayesha wouldn't release her until she was safely upstairs.

Tremaine helped Tracey up.

"Fuck you," she spat. "You're not loyal at all."

"You started this. For what?" He asked.

"Mind your business. Wait till I tell Darius you turned on me!" Tracey screamed.

Tremaine handed her a towel. "I'm done with drama and bullshit. Whatever beef you have with Brielle ends today." He walked inside. Tracey, knowing when Tremaine meant business, wrapped the towel around her arm and followed.

Chapter Twenty-Three

Tremaine located the girls in Brielle's room. He locked the door behind him, taking a moment to study Brielle. She looked like a wounded animal—fragile, yet fierce. Eventually, when they strike back, watch out.

"You okay?" Ayesha asked, trying to comfort Brielle. Her face was bruised, one eye swollen, her lip cut.

"I'm sorry I ruined your party," Brielle sobbed.

A knock at the door made her jump.

"Who is it?" Tremaine asked.

"The owner of this house," Keri replied from the other side.

Tremaine unlocked the door, and his mother came in, Tracey right behind her. Keri turned and shoved Tracey ahead of her into the room.

"I don't know what the hell is going on, but I'm not going to tolerate disrespect. Who started that outside?" Keri's tone left no room for argument. "Somebody better answer me."

"I'm sorry. This is my sister, and we were just having a sisterly fight," Tracey said.

"Well, it looks like your sister won this one. Sit your ass over there," Keri told her. "I'm going to get something for that cut. When I come back, this better be resolved. Peace in my house." She walked out.

"I don't have anything to say to you," Brielle spat.

"That's fine, but I have something to say," Tracey responded as she stepped closer. Tremaine moved to stand beside Brielle, protective.

"I don't hate you. I hate myself. I made bad choices. I ran away at ten. I sold drugs and my body. And now...I'm paying for it all." Tears flowed. "I'm dying, Brielle. I have an incurable disease, and before I go, I needed you to know the truth.

Brielle's anger faded, replaced by shock and concern.

Tremaine held her close. "T, it's okay. I've got your sister. I'm not going to let anything happen to her."

"Based on what?" Tracey's voice rose. "Last time I checked, you were still in the streets!" Tremaine stepped back to let the siblings speak.

"Don't act like you care now!" Brielle shouted. "You were ready to cut me five minutes ago!"

"I do care. I was jealous of you." Tracey admitted.

"What are you talking about?" Brielle yelled.

"You might as well know. We don't share the same father. Mommy didn't know who your father was. My dad told me when I was ten." I felt it was so unfair that my dad loved you more than me."

Brielle broke down, and Ayesha held her, trying to comfort her. She felt completely lost.

"When Jordan tried to hurt me, mama didn't care!" Brielle cried.

Tracey glared. "She did care. She called the cops on him. He was a predator long before you came along. You were her precious baby, and she protected you."

"Did Jordan try to hurt you, too?" Brielle asked with concern in her voice.

"Yes. He did. I was your age—five years old—and it kept happening. That's why I ran away. He and mama stole my childhood," Tracey yelled.

Brielle felt a wave of compassion. She wanted to close this chapter of her life and finally understand her family.

"Where are Jordan and mama?" Brielle asked.

"Jordan's gone. He was caught and later killed in prison. Mama…she's looking for you. Alive, drug-free for five years. I hear about her through the streets."

"I don't want anything to do with her," Brielle said, angry.

"I shouldn't have left you," Tracey admitted, hugging her. "I had to protect myself since no one else would. I love you, and I'm sorry. Seeing you today, all my anger came out."

Brielle, exhausted from the drama, nodded. "Apology accepted."

"Before I go, can I ask a favor?" Tracey asked. Brielle, wary but willing, listened.

"Please…just promise me you'll take care of yourself. Learn from my mistakes. Don't run these streets. Live your life better than I did. That's all I ask."

"Okay," Brielle said softly.

Tracey looked at Tremaine. "Take care of my sister, or I'll kick your ass! And remember…I'm out of the game." She left the room.

Tremaine shook his head, stunned by everything he had just heard. "What the fuck is going on here?" He muttered to himself.

Chapter Twenty-Four

Tremaine looked at Ayesha. "Sis, go back to your party. I got Brielle."

"I don't want to leave her," Ayesha insisted.

"Please, return to your guests," Brielle said softly. "It's okay."

Ayesha kissed her forehead. "I love you, sis," she whispered before leaving.

"A lot has happened today," Tremaine said. "I think we both need to fall back and just chill out."

"I agree," Brielle whispered.

Tremaine glanced over at her, voice lower now. "I'm heading back to my place. You coming or you about to argue with me first?"

Brielle gave him a tired side eye. "Please… I don't even have the energy to argue tonight."

"So, is that a yes?" He pressed.

She nodded, already looking drained. "Yeah. I'm coming."

"Thought so," he muttered.

He laced his fingers through hers and guided her toward the basement stairs. "We going out through the garage. I'm not in the mood to see nobody else tonight."

"Honestly? Same," Brielle said softly.

They moved quietly through the basement and out to the garage, the earlier chaos still hanging in the air between them.

Once they got in the car, Brielle sank back into the seat like her body had finally given up.

Tremaine started the engine.

She let out a long, heavy breath. "Today was...a lot."

"No kidding," he said, pulling out.

Brielle tried to keep her eyes open. Tried being the key word.

Her head tilted toward the window.

Blink.

Blink slower.

By the time Tremaine glanced over at the next light, she was completely out, breathing soft and even in the passenger seat.

He glanced over at her sleeping, thinking about everything that had happened. He admired her strength, resilience, and spirit. He was starting to realize that his feelings for Brielle were deeper than he had expected.

Driving in silence, he reflected on his choice to leave the streets behind. "I can't believe I really got out," he muttered to himself. Looking over at Brielle, he felt a surge of protective affection. He knew he wanted a future with her. One built on trust, love, and family.

Back at his house, he carried her inside, careful not to wake her. He tucked her into bed, making sure she was comfortable. Sitting on the edge of the bed, he whispered a quiet prayer that the drama was finally over.

But just as the house settled into silence, noise erupted downstairs. A loud thud echoed from downstairs.

Brielle's eyes flew open.

She shot upright, heart pounding. "What was that?"

Another noise followed, heavier this time.

And downstairs, someone was definitely trying to get in…unaware they were at the wrong house on the wrong night.

****
****

"This dude living large while we're starving out here," one said, laughing as they broke a window and climbed inside.

Tremaine's sharp instincts kicked in. He grabbed his gun and quietly instructed Brielle to stay put.

"I'm not leaving you," she said.

Tremaine's jaw tightened as another loud thump echoed from downstairs.

Whoever was in his house was moving bold…and sloppy.

He shook his head slowly. "They really don't know who house this is," he muttered.

Beside him, Brielle was already tense, eyes wide but focused.

Tremaine glanced at her, conflicted. Every instinct in him said keep her upstairs, keep her out the way.

But Brielle was already reaching for her phone.

"What you doing?" He asked low.

"I'm calling Twin," she whispered quickly. "Something ain't right."

Before he could argue, she spoke urgently into the phone. "Twin, something's going on. Please come help Tremaine."

She hung up and looked toward the door.

Tremaine caught her wrist lightly. "Stay behind me when we go down there."

Her chin lifted. "I wasn't planning to run."

"I'm serious, Brielle."

"And so am I," she shot back. "I'm not leaving you to handle this by yourself."

For a split second, irritation flashed across his face…but so did something softer.

"Come on," he muttered.

They moved together, slow and careful, heading downstairs step by step. The house creaked under their feet. Tension thick with every stair they took.

Voices drifted from the living room.

Drawers opening.

Things shifting.

Amateurs.

By the time they reached the bottom step, Tremaine's whole

energy had gone cold and controlled.

Two men stood in the middle of his living room, looking around like they had all the time in the world.

They turned when they heard movement.

One of them smirked. "Oh…we got company."

Tremaine stepped forward slightly, positioning himself just ahead of Brielle without making it obvious.

"What y'all looking for?" He asked, voice calm but edged.

The taller one lifted his chin. "Whatever you got."

Brielle's fingers curled tight at her sides, but she stayed planted behind Tremaine just like he told her.

Tremaine's gaze didn't move.

"You picked the wrong house tonight," he said quietly.

And just like that…

The air turned dangerous.

Brielle huddled in the corner, watching him, heart pounding. She had never seen Tremaine like this before—calm, deadly serious, a man fully in control.

One of the intruders laughed nervously. "Man, he's bluffing."

Tremaine tilted his head slightly, eyes locking on the man. "You think I am? Go ahead, make your move."

Tremaine's attitude set the shorter dude off.

"Yo, take this asshole's head off," he snapped at the other one.

Tremaine shook his head. They were talking too much. If they weren't going to move, he would.

He lunged forward and punched the man who had the gun in his face. The impact sent him stumbling backward, and the gun slid across the floor.

The shorter one let out a panicked scream. "That's my brother!"

He charged Tremaine. Brielle screamed.

The front door flew open. Twin rushed in, drawn by the noise. Without hesitation, he pistol-whipped the man, knocking him off Tremaine.

"You good?" Twin asked, breathing hard.

"I'm straight. What the hell you doing here?" Tremaine said, pushing himself up.

"Doesn't matter," Twin replied, turning toward the two men. "Who the fuck are they?"

"No idea," Tremaine said coldly. "But we're about to find out."

Twin glanced at Brielle. She was shaking. He crossed the room and wrapped an arm around her.

"You okay?"

She nodded, unable to speak.

Twin guided her into the kitchen to put space between her and the chaos. He already knew what was coming next—and she'd seen more than enough tonight.

Chapter Twenty-Five

Twin stepped back into the living room. Tremaine had both men pinned against the wall, their hands raised, fear written all over their faces.

"Who the fuck sent y'all to my house?" Tremaine growled.

Silence.

"Don't all answer at once," he said, stepping closer.

Before anyone could react, Tremaine pistol-whipped the shorter one. The crack of bone echoed through the room as the man dropped to the floor clutching his jaw.

He turned to the taller one, pressing the gun to his head.

"Speak before I blow your ass to pieces."

"Nobody sent us," the man cried. "We heard you left the game. We just wanted to make sure you never came back. We had this chick you used to mess with follow you. She gave us everything."

Tremaine smirked.

"Hmph. They say you can't trust a big butt and a smile."

The situation almost amused him. Almost.

But he knew what had to be done. The streets demanded a

lesson.

He fired. One shot. The shorter one never felt it.

The taller one dropped to his knees. "Please, don't kill me. I'm only seventeen."

"Seventeen?" Tremaine said coldly. "You should've thought about that before stepping into a grown man's game."

Another shot rang out.

Silence.

"When it comes to the streets," Twin muttered, "it's kill or be killed."

Twin looked around. "What you gonna do about this mess?"

"Let the cops deal with it," Tremaine said calmly. "This is my house. I defended myself."

He looked at Twin. "Go be with your wife. She could pop any minute."

"Be safe, bro," Twin said before heading out.

Tremaine went into the kitchen. Brielle sat at the table, shaking, tears streaming down her face.

"I'm sorry you had to see that, baby," he said softly.

"I can't do this anymore!" She screamed. "What the fuck is going on?"

He reached for her. She shoved him away.

"Stay the fuck away from me. You almost got us killed. For what? Street bullshit? When are you really gonna leave the game alone?"

"I did leave," he snapped. "That's why this happened. They wanted my spot. They can have it!"

"I don't believe you," she said through tears. "This isn't going to work."

"What you mean?"

"Us. I'm fooling myself thinking you'll ever really change."

His temper flared.

"So you giving up on me? Cool. I don't need a fake bitch, anyway."

The second the words left his mouth, regret hit him.

She turned and walked away from him.

Tremaine cursed under his breath and called 911. After explaining the situation, he heard the front door slam. Brielle was gone.

Five minutes later, the police arrived. His house became a crime scene. He was told to leave.

"When can I come back?" He yelled.

"We'll call you."

He drove straight to his mother's house.

"Ain't this about a bitch," he muttered.

Chapter Twenty-Six

When Tremaine arrived at his mother's house, it was almost five in the morning. Brielle's car wasn't in the driveway.

"Where the fuck could she be?" He muttered, letting himself in with his key. He headed upstairs to Ayesha's room. She was sound asleep. He shook her. She stirred. He shook her harder.

"What the fuck!" She hollered, jumping awake.

"You have to help me find Brielle," he said urgently.

"What do you mean? Where is she, Tremaine?" Ayesha panicked.

"If I knew, I wouldn't be here," he said, pacing. "Where did she stay before she moved in here?"

"I know she lived with her aunt."

"Do you know where exactly?"

"Yeah, but that part of town is not safe at all."

"Get up," he said, pulling her out of bed. "Take me there. She is not safe walking around alone."

"What the fuck happened?" She whispered as she got dressed.

"Some little dudes tried to get at me while we were at my house. Brielle got upset and left."

"We have to find her!" Ayesha screamed.

"No shit. Let's go."

The siblings rushed downstairs and out the house and got in Brielle's car. Ayesha drove in silence toward Brielle's aunt's area. Halfway there, they noticed Tremaine's car parked in front of an abandoned building.

Ayesha parked, and they approached the car. As expected, it had been broken into. Luxury cars in the hood never lasted long. But Tremaine barely flinched.

He got inside, removed his important documents from the glove compartment, and assessed the damage: tires gone, radio stripped.

"Damn," Ayesha muttered.

"Where does she live?" He asked.

"Apartment two, in that building," Ayesha said, pointing.

"I need to find her," Tremaine said, sprinting toward the building with Ayesha right behind him.

The neighborhood was even worse than he remembered. Fiends wandered the streets, the smell of desperation thick in the air.

He ran up the stairs, stopped at apartment two, and knocked firmly. No answer. He banged harder.

Finally, Brielle opened the door, knife in hand, wearing a bathrobe and a scarf on her head.

"What are you doing here?" She asked, surprised.

"I've been looking for you," Tremaine said, his voice tight. "And damn…I didn't mean what I said earlier. Callin' you a bitch—that was wrong. But give me some credit—I've never been here before. Loving someone like this…being in a real relationship…I don't know how to do it right. But I'm willing to learn. Tell me what you need."

Brielle shook her head, tears threatening to fall. "You think words can fix all this? You don't know what it's been like for me, Tremaine. Living here, feeling trapped, carrying…everything."

He stepped closer, brushing a strand of hair from her face. "Then tell me. I'm listening. I'll do whatever it takes."

She swallowed hard, her voice barely above a whisper. "I…I can't do this anymore. I can't live in this chaos. And…I think I might be pregnant."

Tremaine froze, his chest tightening. "Pregnant?"

"I—I don't know for sure," she admitted, trembling. "I just…I haven't gotten my period, and I can't stop worrying. I can't do this alone."

His hands cupped her face, thumbs brushing her cheeks as he searched her eyes. "Brielle…you are never alone. I'm right here. Whatever's coming, we face it together. You hear me?"

She let out a shaky breath, leaning into him. "I'm scared," she whispered.

"I know," he said, pulling her close, wrapping his arms around her. "Me too. But we'll figure it out. Together. Always."

From the doorway, Ayesha called out with a grin, trying to lighten the tension. "Pregnant, huh? About time you made him grow up! Someone's finally taking responsibility."

Brielle laughed through her tears. "Ayesha! Stop it."

"Hey, I'm just saying what we're all thinking," Ayesha teased. "You've got a man who's stubborn enough to protect you…and scared enough to love you right."

Tremaine chuckled, nuzzling Brielle's hair. "Ayesha, mind your business."

"Never," Ayesha shot back, smirking. "But seriously, look at you two. Finally together. Finally honest."

Brielle tilted her head, brushing her lips against Tremaine's. "I love you…but I'm terrified."

He kissed her forehead, then her nose, and lingered on her lips. "Messy, huh? That's love. Real love. And I promise…no more chaos. Not for us. Tonight, we leave. Fresh start. New place. You in?"

Her tears fell freely now, but she smiled, heart pounding. "Yes…with you."

He lifted her in a tight hug, spinning her slightly, and kissed her again—slow, lingering, full of promise. "Good. We'll figure everything else later. For now…just you and me."

Finally, Tremaine pulled back slightly and rested his forehead against hers. "Alright…let's get the hell out of here. Fresh start, new place, and no more chaos," he said with a small, reassuring smile.

Brielle nodded, drawing courage from his presence. She didn't know what the future held, but with Tremaine by her side, she felt ready to face it—whatever it might be.

Chapter Twenty-Seven

After dropping Ayesha back at his mom's house, Tremaine didn't waste time. He booked a hotel room for him and Brielle. Both of them needed a minute to just breathe.

The second they walked in, Brielle kicked off her shoes and tossed her bag onto the bed.

"I cannot believe we're really doing this," she said, half laughing as she flopped down.

Tremaine stretched beside her and nudged her shoulder. "Doing what? Escaping the madness…or being stuck with me for a whole week?"

She rolled her eyes. "Please. Both."

He smirked, but his attention snapped back when Brielle suddenly sat up.

"Hold on," she said.

"What now?" He asked, watching her dig through her bag.

She pulled out a small box and held it up.

Tremaine froze. "…Brielle."

"I just want to check before we leave," she said quickly, already backing toward the bathroom. "And don't start."

"I'm not starting," he muttered, though his whole body had gone tight.

The bathroom door closed.

The longest few minutes of his life crawled by.

When the door finally opened, Brielle stepped out slowly, the test in her hand. Her face was…complicated.

Tremaine stood up. "Talk to me."

She looked down at the test…then back at him.

Her voice came soft. "It's positive."

Silence filled the room.

Tremaine blinked once. Twice. "You serious?"

Brielle let out a shaky breath, nerves and emotion mixing all over her face. "I wouldn't be standing here playing with you."

For a second, he just stared at her like the words were still trying to land.

Then he ran a hand over his face. "Wow…"

Brielle's guard went up a little. "That 'wow' better be a good wow, Tremaine."

His head snapped up. "Girl, stop." He stepped closer, voice rougher now. "I'm just…processing."

She searched his face. "You mad?"

He let out a short breath. "Mad? Nah." His eyes softened as they dropped to the test, then back to her. "Just wasn't expecting my life to change before this Puerto Rico trip."

Despite herself, Brielle huffed out a small laugh. "You stupid."

That broke the tension.

Tremaine closed the space between them and pulled her into his arms, holding her tighter than usual.

"You okay?" He asked quietly near her ear.

Her voice wobbled just a little. "I think so… I'm just…scared and happy at the same time."

"Yeah," he murmured. "Me too."

She leaned back to look at him. "So what we doing now, daddy?"

He snorted. "First of all…relax."

She smiled through the nerves.

His hand slid gently to her stomach, his expression turning serious in a way she hadn't seen before.

"Ain't nothing changing about me taking care of you," he said firmly. "If anything…I'm locked in even more now."

Brielle's eyes softened.

"And my virgin rum punch?" She teased lightly, resting her hand over his.

Tremaine smirked. "Definitely still happening. No alcohol for you, remember?"

She laughed softly and rested her head against his chest again.

"You really be spoiling me," she murmured.

"Only the best for you," he said, pressing a slow kiss to her temple…then glancing down once more at her stomach like reality was still settling in.

And just like that…

This trip meant something very different now.

Her hand instinctively went to her stomach, a mix of nerves and excitement. "I can't believe I'm already thinking about all the baby stuff even on vacation," she whispered.

"It's okay," he said, wrapping his arm around her. "We'll figure it out together. For now, let's just relax…enjoy this."

She tilted her head up, smiling. "Okay, but only if you promise no surprises that make me worry."

"I swear," he said, capturing her lips in a playful kiss. "Just us and the start of something amazing."

The plane touched down in San Juan, and Tremaine couldn't hide his grin as he grabbed Brielle's hand. "Welcome to paradise," he said, his eyes scanning the turquoise water and swaying palms.

"I can't believe we're finally here," Brielle whispered, her fingers intertwined with his. "It already feels like we left all the stress behind."

Tremaine laughed, tugging her toward the cab. "Not a care in the world. Except maybe how many umbrellas you need to shade that gorgeous face of yours."

She rolled her eyes but smiled.

Once they arrived at the resort, Tremaine checked them in while Brielle rested against the balcony railing, taking in the ocean view.

"First order of business," he said, holding up two glasses, "your virgin rum punch."

"Thank you," she said, cradling her drink like it was a treasure.

"You're growing my kid, remember? I've got to keep you healthy and hydrated," he teased, sliding his arm around her shoulders.

She leaned into him, letting out a content sigh. "I'm glad it's just us. No one to stress about. No drama."

"Exactly," he said, pressing a kiss to her temple. "No drama. Just us, the ocean, and maybe a little trouble if you're up for it."

Brielle smirked. "Trouble, huh? What kind?"

"You'll see," he said, leaning closer, letting his lips brush hers in a playful, lingering kiss. "But only if you promise not to run away this time."

"I won't," she whispered, resting her hand over his.

Tremaine's eyes softened. "I love you."

They clinked glasses and let the sun warm them. The sound of waves crashing against the shore masking everything else. For the first time in weeks, neither of them had to think about the streets, the past, or the chaos—they could just be together.

Later that evening, Tremaine and Brielle walked back to their room, toes sandy and spirits high. Tremaine tossed the keys onto the dresser and spun her around.

"So, our first night in paradise…what's the plan?" He asked with a grin.

Brielle laughed, swaying on her heels. "Plan? I was thinking room service, maybe a little music?"

He leaned in and brushed her hair back from her face. "And a little romance, don't forget that."

Brielle's stomach fluttered. She put a hand over her belly, suddenly aware of how delicate this moment felt.

"You okay?" Tremaine asked, noticing her pause.

"Yeah…just…feeling a little full from the drink and food," she admitted.

He smiled and brushed his thumb lightly over her hand on her stomach. "I've got you.

She laughed softly, shaking her head. "You really do make everything feel special."

"And you," he said, cupping her cheek, "make everything worth it."

He leaned in for a slow kiss, gentle and lingering, careful not to crowd her. She melted into him, feeling safe and cherished. The chaos of the world far away.

****
*****

The morning sun spilled through the curtains, warming the room. Brielle stretched, feeling the slight flutter of nerves mixed with excitement. Tremaine was already up, leaning against the balcony railing, coffee in hand, watching the ocean.

"Morning, sleepyhead," he called, grinning when she appeared in a loose sundress.

"Morning," she yawned, walking over. "You're up early."

"Someone has to enjoy this view before the day gets too busy," he said, nudging her gently with his shoulder. "You're coming, right? Beachside breakfast?"

She nodded. "I'll come, but you're carrying my chair this time."

"Chair duty accepted," he teased, pretending to struggle under her weight.

Breakfast was at a small beachside café with fruity drinks for him and her virgin mocktail, and fresh pastries. The waiter offered them a little local delicacy to share. Tremaine winked. "You have to try it. Don't worry, all safe for the mommy to be."

Brielle laughed, taking a cautious bite.

They spent the morning walking along the beach, exploring little coves and hidden paths. Tremaine kept glancing at her belly, occasionally sliding his hand lightly over it, making her smile.

"You know," he said, leaning close so she could hear him over the ocean, "I still can't believe we're doing this. Just us, away from everything…I needed this."

"Me too," Brielle admitted. "It's…peaceful. And with you, it's even better."

He grinned. "Even when I'm annoying?"

She poked his side. "Even when you're annoying."

By midday, they found a small market in the heart of the old town. Tremaine picked up a handmade bracelet and slid it onto her wrist. "A little souvenir," he said, winking. "To remind you that even when things get crazy, you've got me."

"And what about this?" She teased, pointing to her belly.

He looked down at her, smiling softly. "Never forgetting. The baby is already the most important thing in my life. And you. Don't think I've forgotten about you either."

They laughed and joked through the narrow streets, sampling tropical fruit, playing with local vendors' games, and teasing each other when they lost. Brielle couldn't remember the last time she'd laughed this freely.

Later, back at the hotel, Tremaine insisted on carrying her to the pool area. "No arguments," he said firmly, smirking. "I need to protect my girl and my little VIP."

She rolled her eyes, laughing. "VIP, huh? You really like titles."

"Only when they're mine," he replied, settling her in a lounge chair. He handed her a fresh virgin piña colada.

She clinked her glass against his.

"To us," she said softly.

Tremaine grinned, resting his hand lightly on her belly. "To us," he echoed, feeling the flutter beneath his fingers, though she didn't realize it yet.

As the sun dipped lower, they held hands in the pool, floating lazily and teasing each other over silly games. The tension from the past weeks felt like it had melted away, replaced by laughter, intimacy, and a rare sense of calm.

By the end of the day, with sun-kissed skin and salty hair, Tremaine pulled Brielle close as they watched the sunset. "You know," he murmured, "I don't care about all the drama waiting for us at home. Here. Now. It's just us. You, me, and this little one."

Brielle rested her head against his chest, breathing in the warm tropical air. "I like it here," she whispered. "I like us."

"And we're going to keep it this way," he promised, pressing a soft kiss to the top of her head. "No chaos. No stress…just us, for now."

****

Brielle woke to the sound of waves crashing gently against the shore. Tremaine was already up, sprawled across the balcony, sketching little notes in a notebook.

"Morning," she said, stretching and yawning.

"Morning," he replied, looking up with a grin. "Tea? Or do you want me to make you something fancy like yesterday?"

"Tea, and maybe a little pastry?" She teased.

"You drive a hard bargain," he said, hopping to his feet and wrapping her in a quick hug. "But I'll survive."

Breakfast was at a small café tucked into the colorful streets of

Old San Juan. Tremaine ordered a fresh tropical juice for himself and a green tea for Brielle, nodding toward her belly.

She laughed. "I feel like a pregnant queen," she teased, brushing a strand of hair from her face.

He studied her for a second, a slow smile creeping onto his face. "You glowing, you know that?"

Brielle rolled her eyes, but her hand drifted instinctively to her stomach. "Boy, don't start."

"I'm serious," he said, leaning back in his chair. "If I didn't know no better, I'd say we got a little somebody already making their presence known."

Her stomach flipped, nerves and emotion mixing together. She tried to play it off. "You so extra."

Tremaine reached across the table and caught her hand before she could pull it away, his grip warm and steady.

"You nervous?" He asked softly.

She hesitated, then gave a small shrug. "A little…yeah."

His thumb brushed gently over her knuckles. "Hey," he murmured, eyes locked on hers. "You good. We good."

Brielle's expression softened despite herself.

He gave her hand a light squeeze, a hint of that familiar smirk returning. "And for the record…this little glow you got going on?"

She lifted a brow. "What about it?"

"I like it," he said simply. "I like you."

Her lips tried not to smile.

Tried…and failed.

After breakfast, they wandered through the streets, playing with the colorful tiles and vibrant architecture. Tremaine kept teasing her whenever she stumbled or hesitated.

"Careful," he said, catching her hand. "I need my favorite girl in one piece."

"I'm fine!" She shot back, trying not to laugh.

"Are you, though?" He pressed, brushing a strand of hair behind her ear. His fingers lingered just a moment longer than necessary.

She shivered slightly unaware it wasn't just the breeze. "I'm fine," she repeated, but her smile betrayed her.

By midday, they found a quiet terrace overlooking the bay. Tremaine ordered some fresh seafood while Brielle stuck to her virgin drink, reminding him each sip that it had to be safe.

They spent the rest of the afternoon walking along the beach, splashing in the shallow water, teasing each other about who was the better swimmer. Every touch, every laugh, drew them closer. The past stress and tension felt like a distant memory as they floated in the warmth of each other's company.

As the sun dipped low, Tremaine wrapped his arms around her from behind, resting his chin on her shoulder. "You know," he murmured, "I don't care what comes after this trip. For now…this is perfect. You, me, and a little one on the way."

Brielle shivered at the thought, pressing her hand against her stomach, a mix of nerves and excitement curling in her chest. He kissed the top of her head as they watched the sunset paint the sky in shades of gold and pink.

The last evening in San Juan, Brielle and Tremaine sat on the balcony again, the city lights twinkling below and the ocean stretching endlessly before them. The air was warm, salty, and perfect.

Tremaine nudged her playfully. "So, we survived our first vacation without killing each other or anyone else. Not bad, right?"

Brielle laughed, leaning into him. "Barely. But I have to admit…this was exactly what we needed."

He tilted his head, studying her. "You sure about that?"

"About what?"

"That you're ready for the next chapter," he said softly, brushing his thumb over her hand. His gaze lingered on her stomach, and she shifted slightly, noticing his look.

"I…I don't know," she whispered, unsure herself.

"Hey," he said, pulling her close, "We got this. You and me, like we promised. No running. No hiding. Just us."

Brielle took a deep breath. The thought of a new city, a fresh start, and a baby with him felt both terrifying and exhilarating. "I want that," she said finally.

Tremaine's face broke into a relieved grin. "Good. Because

I've been thinking…it's time to lock this down. New city. New life. Just us, building something real."

Her heart pounded. "Even…with a baby?"

He chuckled, brushing a strand of hair from her face. "Especially with a baby. We'll figure it out, Brielle. No matter what."

She laughed, half out of nerves, half out of excitement. "You really think we can do this?"

He kissed her forehead, then pressed his lips to hers. "I know we can. Together."

They held each other as the waves rolled in below, the sun setting on the horizon. For the first time in a long time, neither of them felt chaos or danger pressing in. Just hope, possibility, and a life they were ready to fight for—together.

Chapter Twenty-Eight

By the time they were headed back to the States, Puerto Rico was still wrapped around them like a warm memory neither one of them was ready to shake.

On the flight home, Brielle stayed tucked against Tremaine's shoulder, quieter than usual. The steady hum of the plane had her calm in a way he hadn't seen in a minute.

His hand moved slow along her back, careful, protective without making a big deal about it.

"You real quiet over there," he murmured.

She didn't lift her head. "Just thinking."

"Uh oh," he teased lightly. "That never sound safe."

Brielle gave a soft huff. "I'm serious."

He glanced down at her. "Talk to me."

She hesitated, then spoke low. "I been thinking about…everything. Us. The baby." Her fingers rested over her stomach. "What if we really just… leave all this behind?"

Tremaine's hand slid over hers instantly, his grip warm and sure.

"I ain't mad at that kind of thinking," he said, a small grin pulling at his mouth. "New city. Fresh start. Nobody in our business." He leaned his head lightly against hers. "Just you, me…and our little plus one."

Brielle let out a nervous laugh, but her eyes were shiny. "You say it so easy."

"It's not easy," he said honestly. "But it's doable."

She finally looked up at him. "I'm scared, Tremaine."

He smirked a little. "You supposed to be. Just don't be scared of the wrong stuff." His thumb brushed over her hand. "We handle things one step at a time. Like we always do."

By the time they landed, the soft moment had shifted into planning mode.

Tremaine pulled out his phone as they walked through the airport. "Matter fact…I been looking at houses."

Brielle blinked. "Already?"

He turned the screen toward her. "I don't play when I make up my mind. Look. Something with space. Yard. Quiet block. Good schools nearby…you know…just in case."

Her chest tightened in the best and scariest way.

"You really serious about this," she said softly.

Tremaine stopped walking and looked straight at her. "I told you. I'm done running. Done with chaos. I mean that."

Something in his voice made her believe him.

For real this time.

Later, when they finally made it back to Tremaine's house,

Brielle sank onto the bed, emotionally and physically worn out.

But her heart felt…lighter.

She leaned her head against his shoulder again, voice barely above a whisper.

"I like the sound of that life you talking about."

Tremaine slid his arm around her, pulling her close.

"Get used to it," he murmured.

And for the first time in a long time, Brielle let herself sit in the feeling.

Hope.

Quiet.

And maybe…finally safe.

****
*****

He was making the final preparations when Brielle came into the room and slapped him in the face. "I fucking hate your lying ass," she spat, throwing some papers at him.

Tremaine was confused at her outburst. He picked the papers up and began to read.

Dear Little sister,

If you are reading this then I am no longer with you. I want you to know the truth about everything that has occurred in your life so far. I know everything has not been peaches and cream with us. I don't hate you. In fact, I am jealous of you. I couldn't believe how mama had Jordan arrested when he tried to touch you but did nothing when he raped me. I was mad at you for my father leaving the house. He left because he couldn't stand looking at you. You are a product of mama's thirst for crack. No one knows who your dad is. I'm sorry to be telling you that but it is the truth.

I didn't know that you knew Tremaine. Please be careful with him. He is nothing but a street dude that doesn't value women. I know because Tremaine, Twin, Darius, and I all grew up together. Running the streets with the boys made me realize that they are nothing but dogs. You have been warned.

I want you to forgive me for everything. I didn't want to leave you, but I was tired of being abused day in and day out by that bastard, Jordan. I was tired of mama taking her anger out on me when she couldn't get a fix. So, I ran away, me and Darius, our cousin. I wanted to take you but you were only five. The streets are no joke. I don't want you to be with Tremaine. He is not going to leave the streets for you and if you believe that, you are a damn fool.

I love you and I want you to be better than me and mama. I want you to pursue your dreams.

I love you and please be safe out here.

Love,

Your big sister Tracey

"What the fuck" Tremaine said, stunned at the letter's contents. "Where did you get this?" He asked.

"It doesn't matter where I got it from," Brielle snapped, her voice already shaking. Her eyes were glossy, frantic. "Just tell me the truth. Are Tracey and Darius cousins?"

Tremaine hesitated.

And her whole face broke.

Her hand flew to her mouth. "Oh my God…" Her voice rose, cracking wide open. "Is my sister dead? Tremaine, is she dead?"

He stepped toward her quickly. "Brielle, listen to me. If that part is true, I didn't know. I swear I didn't know." His voice was tight. "I knew they was too close, yeah…but I didn't know all that."

The room started spinning.

Brielle stumbled back like the air had been knocked out of her chest.

"No…no, this can't be real…" Her breathing turned ragged. Then her hands dropped to her stomach, trembling. "Oh my God…"

Tremaine's phone started ringing.

Neither of them moved at first.

He ignored it, eyes locked on her as she started to come apart.

"Aren't you going to answer that?" She asked, but her voice was thin now…breaking.

"No," he said softly, stepping closer. "I'm worried about you right now—"

He reached for her.

She slapped his hand away, harder this time.

"Don't touch me!" She screamed, tears spilling fast now. "You don't understand!"

The phone rang again.

Louder.

More urgent.

Her whole body started shaking. "I was violated, Tremaine!" She cried, the words ripping out of her chest. "That man…that man is my cousin!"

Tremaine froze.

Her hands pressed protectively over her stomach, panic flooding her face. she sobbed.

Her voice broke completely.

"I can't…I can't breathe…" she choked, pacing now, spiraling. "My sister is gone, my family is twisted, and I got a whole baby growing inside me"

The phone rang again.

Sharp.

Relentless.

She turned on him, eyes red and furious and shattered all at once.

"Answer the damn phone!" She screamed, her voice echoing through the room.

Because deep down…

She already knew nothing about this situation was about to get easier.

The phone kept ringing. Frustrated, Tremaine reached in his pocket to turn it off. Before he did, he glanced at the screen to see who was calling him back-to-back. It was Twin.

"Something's wrong?" Brielle asked, sensing something wasn't right.

Ignoring her, Tremaine called Twin back.

He didn't even get to say anything before Twin said, "Yo, get to Newark Hospital right now!"

"What the fuck happened?" Tremaine immediately thought the worse.

"T. tried to rob Snake, and his goons got at her."

"What the fuck?" Tremaine yelled. "I'm coming right now."

After hanging up, he started putting on his sneakers.

Brielle watched his face shift and immediately frowned. "What now? What's wrong with you?"

Tremaine was already moving, tension written all over him. "I gotta step out for a minute."

Her eyes narrowed fast. "Excuse me?"

"Just stay here," he said, grabbing his keys. His voice was calm, but she knew that tone. Something was brewing. "I'll be back. And don't open this door for nobody."

Brielle let out a sharp, tired laugh. "Oh, so now I'm on lockdown too?"

He stepped closer and pressed a quick kiss to her forehead like he was trying to soften the blow. "I mean it, Brielle."

And just like that…he was gone.

The door clicked shut behind him.

Silence filled the room.

Brielle stood there for a second, staring at the door like it personally offended her.

"Unbelievable," she muttered, dragging a hand down her face. "Just…unbelievable."

Between the mess with Tracey, the drama with Darius, and now Tremaine walking out mid-argument, her nerves were officially shot.

"Yeah…today can go straight in the trash," she grumbled.

Her body finally gave in to the exhaustion she'd been fighting all day. She kicked off her shoes, crawled into the bed, and dropped back against the pillows.

"I am so tired of this foolishness," she whispered to herself.

Within minutes, the weight of the day pulled her under, frustration still written all over her face even as sleep finally claimed her.

****
****

What the fuck was Tracey thinking? Tremaine wondered as he sped to the hospital.

Snake was an invincible big man who always carried his burner with him. No one thought to cross him because they knew the consequences were deadly. Tracey knew how Snake was, so Tremaine didn't understand why she would try to cross him. Being in the drug game, you learn who to run over and who not to fuck around with.

Once he entered the neighborhood where the hospital was located, he slowed down his speed. He didn't need to get arrested. When he reached the parking lot, he pulled up beside Twin's Mercedes. Twin and Tracey used to mess around back in the day. He had mad love for her.

When Tremaine walked into the hospital, he saw Twin. With a look of sadness, Twin stood up.

"She's gone, man," Twin said softly.

Tremaine shook his head. "Brielle got some letter saying that she was dead. What the fuck is going on. When did this happen!" Tremaine demanded.

"I heard about it in the streets."

"Why did she do what she did?" Tremaine questioned.

"I don't know why" She died from being stabbed multiple times. That's the word in the streets."

"This is some bullshit, homie," Tremaine said, hitting the wall.

"Chill, son. Here comes the doctor now."

The doctor came over to the two friends. "We need someone to identify the body. Are you family?"

"No, but I can get her sister," Tremaine told him.

"That's fine. My name is Dr. Shaps. Just ask for me, and I'll come get you."

"Thank you, doctor," Tremaine said.

He hurried to his car with Twin right behind him. Twin headed home while he headed to confirm to Brielle what she already knew.

Tremaine hung up and drove in silence, shedding tears for his dead homie. Tracey had guts to do what she did, and though he was heartbroken, he couldn't be mad at Snake. The streets lived by one code: death before dishonor. Growing up with Tracey, Twin, and Darius, Tremaine had learned the game cold. He carried a burner, kept minimal company, and never let anyone in.

By the time he pulled up to his house, Brielle was standing outside. He got out to walk over to her.

"What the fuck, Tremaine!" She yelled, running up to him and hitting him.

"I'm not joking," he said, grabbing her arms. "Chill the fuck out and let's go."

"So, the letter is true?!" She sobbed.

"Let's go," he repeated. When she didn't move, he gently shoved her toward the car.

"Yo, Brielle, shut the fuck up!" He barked, frustrated by her crying.

She stayed silent after that, but tears streamed down her face. Her sister couldn't be gone. she had seen her just days ago.

Tremaine rubbed her thigh in an attempt to comfort her, silently wishing he could take away her pain. He wanted nothing more than to get her to the hospital safely and bring her back home.

Once in the parking lot, he helped her out of the car. She leaned into him as he hugged her tightly.

"I'm here for you, baby," he whispered, kissing her forehead.

Brielle drew strength from his presence and whispered, "I'm ready."

Tremaine led her into the hospital and got the front desk to contact the doctor while Brielle sat in the corner, reflecting. Her life had never been easy. When she left home for good at five, she only learned about Tracey later while living with Aunt Sarah. Tracey had always tormented her, flaunting designer clothes and teasing Brielle mercilessly. By eighteen, Brielle had left, tried jobs that didn't stick, stripped for survival, and enrolled in college—all while saving every dime she could.

Now, at twenty-two, her life felt shattered. She had love for Tremaine, but it wasn't enough. She wanted safety, stability, and security. Things she feared Tremaine couldn't give while still tied to the streets.

Little did she know, Tremaine had truly left the game. He had plans for a legitimate life. All he wanted now was a chance at real love.

Dr. Shap appeared, ready to lead them to Tracey's body. Brielle froze, terrified, and Tremaine took her hand.

When they entered the room, Brielle's sobs broke free at the sight of her sister.

"Who did this?" She cried.

"Is this your sister, ma'am?" Dr. Shap asked gently, ignoring the question.

"Yes," Brielle sobbed, and Tremaine held her close, letting her grief pour out.

"We can hold the body for up to a week while you make arrangements. I have some of her belongings to give you," the doctor said, handing Brielle a bag. "I'm sorry for your loss."

Brielle took the bag and walked out silently.

"We'll come back during the week. Thanks," Tremaine said, following her.

"Get me out of here, please," she whispered.

"Alright," he said, not wanting to argue.

He handed her the keys, and she quickly walked out the hospital. Brielle didn't wait for him. She pulled off immediately.

"What the fuck! This bitch done stole my car!" Tremaine muttered, frustration boiling over. For years, he'd heard men claim women were nothing but trouble. Now, he felt it firsthand.

It was almost midnight, and there was only person he knew to call that would be up: Darius.

"Yo, what's good, my dude?"

"I need you to come get me," Tremaine said, voice flat.

Darius frowned. "Why you sound like that? Where you at?"

"The hospital."

A beat of silence. "The hospital? What the hell you doing there?"

Tremaine's patience snapped. "Just pull up."

Click.

A few minutes later, Darius's horn cut through the night.

Tremaine slid into the passenger seat without a word.

Darius took one look at him and leaned back. "Yeah…you definitely look like you been through it."

"Drive," Tremaine muttered. "Take me to my mom's."

Darius pulled off, the usual jokes dying on his lips when he peeped Tremaine's mood.

"Aight," he said carefully. "You gonna tell me what's going on, or we just riding in silence?"

Tremaine stared straight ahead.

"Tracey's dead."

The car went real quiet.

Darius's hands tightened on the wheel. "T?" His voice dropped. "When? How that happen?"

"She tried to rob Snake."

"What the hell?" Darius barked. "She know better than that. Snake don't play."

"She wasn't thinking about herself," Tremaine said low. "She was thinking about her little sister."

Darius frowned immediately. "Little sister? Tracey ain't got no sister."

That made Tremaine finally turn and look at him.

"You and her cousins," he said slowly. "And you ain't know she had a sister?"

Darius shook his head quick. "Nah. Tracey's father my uncle. It was just her and her brother. Her moms was messed up, yeah, but ain't no sister come from my uncle's side."

Tremaine's jaw flexed.

"You know Brielle."

Darius scoffed lightly. "Yeah. Ayesha's little friend. What about her?"

Tremaine held his gaze.

"That's Tracey's sister."

The car drifted slightly before Darius corrected it.

"No," he said immediately. "Nah, that don't even sound right."

"Different fathers," Tremaine said. "Same mother."

Darius let out a dry laugh that had zero humor in it. "You serious right now?"

"I wish I wasn't."

The realization started creeping across Darius's face.

Slow.

Ugly.

"Wait…" His voice dropped. "You saying…she my blood?"

Tremaine didn't answer right away.

And that silence made Darius look at him fully.

Really look.

That's when Tremaine leaned back in the seat, voice going cold.

"I know what you did to her."

Everything in the car froze.

Darius's head snapped toward him. "What?"

Tremaine's eyes were hard now. No guessing. No confusion.

"I know you put your hands on Brielle."

The words landed heavy.

Darius's face drained. "Hold up—"

"Don't," Tremaine cut in sharply. "Don't play stupid with me."

Darius's grip tightened on the wheel, breathing uneven now. "I didn't know who she was," he said quickly. "Tremaine, I swear—"

"That ain't the point," Tremaine snapped, anger finally breaking through. "You still did it."

Silence filled the car except for the low hum of the engine.

Darius dragged a hand over his face, shaken. "If I would've known she was my cousin—"

"You wouldn't have touched her. Yeah, I figured," Tremaine said, voice rough.

Darius finally looked at him fully, guilt and frustration all over his face. "You think I'm proud of that?"

Tremaine leaned closer, voice low and dangerous.

"I'm telling you this once so we clear…if it ever come down to you or her?"

The car rolled to a stop in front of his mother's house.

Tremaine's eyes locked on Darius.

"I'm choosing her."

The words sat heavy between them.

Darius swallowed hard, hurt and disbelief flashing across his face. "After everything we been through?"

"Loyalty don't mean I ignore what you did," Tremaine shot back.

Darius looked straight ahead now, jaw tight. "So that's where we at."

"That's exactly where we at," Tremaine said calmly.

A long, thick silence passed.

Then Darius spoke low. "Don't expect me to forget this."

Tremaine opened the door.

"I don't."

And just like that, he stepped out, leaving the tension burning inside the car.

****

The moment Tremaine stepped out of the car, he already knew Brielle was inside.

He could feel it.

The house was too quiet. Too heavy. Like the walls themselves knew the night had been too long.

He didn't waste time. The second he got in he went straight to the bedroom.

And there she was.

Curled up on the bed, small and tired, eyes red like she hadn't gotten a second of real rest.

She sat up the minute she saw him.

"You talked to him," she said, voice soft but certain.

Tremaine shut the door behind him slowly. "Yeah. I did."

Brielle watched his face close, searching for answers before he even spoke.

"Well?" She asked, nerves creeping back in.

He moved closer to the bed, expression steady but serious. "He knows I know," Tremaine said plainly. "Ain't no confusion no more."

Her breath caught.

"And?" She pressed quietly.

Tremaine reached for her hands and pulled her gently toward him. "And I meant what I said. We not sitting around waiting for more problems to find us."

Her brows pulled together. "What are you saying, Tremaine?"

"I'm saying we moving. Now." he replied. "New place. Clean start. I'm done letting this mess circle us."

Emotion flickered across her face.

"And you…and Darius?" She asked carefully.

Tremaine's jaw tightened once.

"I chose you," he said, calm and firm.

No pause. No hesitation.

The words hit her straight in the chest.

Brielle's face crumbled and she folded into him, pressing her face into his shirt like she'd been holding herself together by a thread.

"I feel like everything just keeps falling apart," she whispered.

Tremaine pulled her in tighter, hand cradling the back of her head.

"Then we build somewhere new," he murmured. "Somewhere all this noise can't reach us so easy."

Outside, the night carried on like nothing had shifted.

But inside that house…

Everything had changed.

"We gotta move. Like… right now," Tremaine said, already on his feet.

Brielle didn't argue.

That alone told him how exhausted she really was.

No attitude. No questions. Just a quiet nod as she slid off the bed and started grabbing what she could.

"Just the important stuff," he said, moving fast and focused.

"I know," she murmured, stuffing the last of her things into her bag.

This wasn't panic.

This was done.

When they stepped outside, the night air hit cool and heavy. Brielle automatically moved closer, and Tremaine pulled her into his side without thinking.

"You holding up?" he asked low.

She rested her hand lightly over her stomach before looking up at him. "Trying to. It's just…a lot."

His hand covered hers without hesitation.

"We got this," he said quietly. "You and the baby…I got y'all."

Her throat tightened, but she nodded.

The cab pulled up.

Tremaine slid in first and pulled her right beside him. She curled into his side like her body had officially clocked out.

"Harlem," he told the driver.

As the city lights blurred past, Brielle's breathing slowly evened out.

Within minutes, she was asleep.

Tremaine stayed awake, staring out the window, mind already ten steps ahead.

Darius.

Snake.

Loose ends that never stayed loose for long.

His arm tightened slightly around Brielle.

Then his eyes dropped briefly to her stomach.

"Yeah," he muttered under his breath. "Everything different now."

When the cab finally stopped, he gently nudged her. "We here, baby."

She blinked awake, groggy but trusting, letting him guide her inside.

At the desk, Diego looked up and grinned. "What's good?"

"Need a room," Tremaine said. "Me and my girl."

"One bed or two?"

"One. For the week."

Diego named the price. Tremaine paid without hesitation.

Upstairs, the room was quiet.

Too quiet.

Tremaine did a quick scan before guiding Brielle to the bed. He crouched and slipped off her sneakers while she curled into herself.

She watched him, voice soft. "So what happens now?"

"Now you rest," he said. "That's step one."

She gave a tired half smile. "And step two, Mr. Planner?"

A faint smirk touched his mouth. "Step two, I go clean out the house in a day or two. Grab what we need. Cars too."

Her brows lifted. "You going back there by yourself?"

"I'll handle it," he said calmly. "You not stepping foot back in that mess. Not right now."

Her hand drifted back to her stomach. "You really serious about all this."

He stepped closer, voice firm and low. "Brielle…everything different now. I'm thinking long game."

She studied him, emotions soft but heavy. "You not going nowhere…right?"

He shook his head once. "Not a chance."

Only then did her shoulders finally relax.

Tremaine checked the locks. The windows. Old habits still riding shotgun.

When he finally slid into bed, Brielle tucked herself into his chest like muscle memory.

His arm wrapped around her automatically.

Outside, the city kept moving.

Inside the room, it was finally quiet.

But Tremaine's eyes stayed open in the dark, thoughts running laps he couldn't shut off.

Darius wasn't done.

Snake definitely wasn't done.

And the streets had a long memory.

His jaw flexed once…then slowly, finally, his body started to give in.

With Brielle warm against him and the weight of everything heavy on his mind, Tremaine's eyes closed.

Sleep took him.